A KILLING IN COMICS

MAX ALLAN COLLINS

BERKLEY PRIME CRIME, NEW YORK

THE BERKLEY PUBLISHING GROUP
Published by the Penguin Group
Penguin Group (USA) Inc.
375 Hudson Street, New York, New York 10014, USA
Penguin Group (Canada), 90 Eglinton Avenue East, Suite 700, Toronto, Ontario M4P 2Y3, Canada
(a division of Pearson Penguin Canada Inc.)
Penguin Books Ltd., 80 Strand, London WC2R 0RL, England
Penguin Group Ireland, 25 St. Stephen's Green, Dublin 2, Ireland
(a division of Penguin Books Ltd.)
Penguin Group (Australia), 250 Camberwell Road, Camberwell, Victoria 3124, Australia
(a division of Pearson Australia Group Pty. Ltd.)
Penguin Books India Pvt. Ltd., 11 Community Centre, Panchsheel Park, New Delhi—110 017, India
Penguin Group (NZ), 67 Apollo Drive, Mairangi Bay, Auckland 1311, New Zealand
(a division of Pearson New Zealand Ltd.)
Penguin Books (South Africa) (Pty.) Ltd., 24 Sturdee Avenue, Rosebank, Johannesburg 2196, South
Africa

Penguin Books Ltd., Registered Offices: 80 Strand, London WC2R 0RL, England

This book is an original publication of The Berkley Publishing Group.

This is a work of fiction. Names, characters, places, and incidents either are the product of the author's imagination or are used fictitiously, and any resemblance to actual persons, living or dead, business establishments, events, or locales is entirely coincidental. The publisher does not have any control over and does not assume any responsibility for author or third-party websites or their content.

PRINTING HISTORY
Berkley Prime Crime trade paperback edition / May 2007

Library of Congress Cataloging-in-Publication Data

Collins, Max Allan.
 A killing in comics / Max Allan Collins. — Berkley Prime Crime trade pbk. ed.
  p. cm.
 ISBN 978-0-425-21365-0
 1. Comic books, strips, etc.—Authorship—Fiction. 2. Cartoonists—Fiction. 3. Manhattan
(New York, N.Y.)—Fiction. I. Title.
 PS3553.O4753K53 2007
 813'.54—dc22   2006038923

PRINTED IN THE UNITED STATES OF AMERICA

10 9 8 7 6 5 4 3 2 1

BERKLEY PRIME CRIME TITLES BY
MAX ALLAN COLLINS

THE TITANIC MURDERS
THE HINDENBURG MURDERS
THE PEARL HARBOR MURDERS
THE LUSITANIA MURDERS
THE LONDON BLITZ MURDERS
THE WAR OF THE WORLDS MURDER
A KILLING IN COMICS

DATE DUE

...NS

"Colli   e's no better
word   hen the out-
come i   er."

                                              nion-Tribune

"Colli   ive and con-
cise, b   *brary Journal*

"No o

                                              air Detective

"An u

                                              Bend Tribune

"When   history in a
way th   better than
Max A   *Chill of Night*

"Proba   has so suc-
cessfully blended real characters and events with fictional ones. The
versatile Collins is an excellent storyteller." —*The Tennessean*

"The master of true-crime fiction." —*Publishers Weekly*

continued . . .

"The author makes history come alive. . . . The details of life, the dialogue and the realities of living in London during wartime are meticulously set out for the reader. The nightly blackouts . . . make the perfect setting for criminal activities. The mystery [is] well crafted and quite interesting. . . . A new Collins novel is a treat for lovers of history and mystery alike."

—*The Romance Readers Connection*

"Entertaining . . . full of colorful characters . . . a stirring conclusion."

—*Detroit Free Press*

"Collins ably weaves a well-paced, closed-environment mystery reminiscent of Agatha Christie. . . . [He] succeeds in . . . reimagining the *Lusitania*'s final voyage."

—*Publishers Weekly*

"Collins makes it sound as though it really happened."

—*New York Daily News*

"Collins does a fine job of insinuating a mystery into a world-famous disaster. . . . [He] manage[s] to raise plenty of goosebumps before the ship goes down for the count."

—*Mystery News*

"[Collins's] descriptions are so vivid and colorful that it's like watching a movie . . . [and he] gives the reader a front row seat."

—*Cozies, Capers & Crimes*

IN MEMORY OF

WILL EISNER

THE SPIRIT OF COMICS

*"They were a generation of boys
who were never adolescents
and yet whose fantasies and emotional lives
were caught at the cusp of adolescence
forever."*

Gerard Jones, Men of Tomorrow

. . . *and, in July of 1948, Manhattan is my town.*

Sure, I have to share this island with a few million others, na-tives and tourists alike, many of whom sleep high up enough to enjoy a cool breeze off the Hudson, cut by boat whistles and the occasional police or fire siren. But if you don't cliff-dwell, or if you're a tourist who can't afford a high-rise hotel, don't sweat it—my town is air-conditioned, from the TV-rigged gin mills to the mink-lined nightspots.

For you outdoor types, I suggest spending a buck-fifty by cab from Times Square to any one of the stadium homes of our three major-league ball clubs. Boxing can be viewed under God's starry ceiling, too—or inside and air-cooled, for you gentle souls, at Madison Square and lesser venues. And Central Park is free, at least before midnight.

Hungry? On the east side, try the Stork Club's chicken

hamburger with tomato sauce a la Walter Winchell, served up with french-fried sweet potatoes and buttered green peas for not much more than what an average Peoria hotel room would stake you. Or if they won't let you in at the Stork (which they probably won't), stop at any Automat and slip in a coin and get back a real burger, quick and hot; or if you like your beef corned and maybe with a slice of Swiss, Reuben's on East Fifty-eighth is the genuine kosher article.

On the west side, four-fifty at Jack Dempsey's will get you a big sirloin steak with french-fried onions, baked potato and house salad; or three bucks, at the Strip Joint on Forty-second, just a block and a half off Broadway, will entitle you to the best NY strip steak in town with the same trimmings. (I recommend the latter, only in part because I have a piece of the action.)

Looking for a view? Try an ear-popper of an elevator ride to the observation deck of the Empire State or the Chrysler Building or maybe Radio City. This works for you depressed types, too—if the magnificence of the cityscape doesn't get your mind off your woes, you can always take a header. That ride, at least, is still free in this man's town.

Entertainment? Broadway serves up a dozen shows and, by mid-July, the flops have all flopped and the hits have all hit. I'd recommend Hank Fonda in Mr. Roberts *at the Alvin Theater and* High Button Shoes *with Phil Silvers at the Shubert, or maybe you might want to watch that kid Brando do his magnificent mumble in* A Streetcar Named Desire, *at the Ethel Barrymore, if you can land a ticket.*

Shopping? I'd have to say Madison Avenue—it's come on strong, the last decade or so, thanks to being situated between Fifth and Park avenues. More intimate shops can be found below Fifty-ninth, everything from flowers to pets, perfumes to paintings, millinery to luggage, period furniture to furniture period.

Now it's pricey, but if you're going to do any of the above, you might want to bunk in at New York's unofficial palace, the Waldorf-Astoria—between Forty-ninth and Fiftieth streets, Park and Lexington avenues. The famous old Waldorf had to get out of the way of the Empire State, but the "new" hotel (1931) has the same old traditions, including Peacock Alley, the Empire Room and the Astor Gallery.

Even New Yorkers are wowed by the Waldorf. The massive limestone and light-brick building spans the tracks of the New York Central, lending privileged guests private railroad sidings. How the building avoids all that rattle and roar, you'll have to ask Schultze and Weaver, who put the thing up—a sheer eighteen stories followed by a series of setbacks topped by twin chrome-crowned towers adding up to fifty stories, give or take.

The interior is impressive, natch—lobby a mile wide, mosaics depicting nude figures, yard after yard of marble and stone and rich wood and nickel bronze, with eighteenth-century English and Early American furnishings, and more paintings by more famous artists than most museums can manage. Two thousand staffers look after guests in as many rooms. But the really toney digs are reserved for the suites in the towers, strictly residential.

You may wonder how a mug like me would even know about such suites. But this story begins in one of them, and a life key to the tale ends there.

Interested?

The fat man in the blue cape and red tights and blue boots was
sweating.

His brow, balding back to yesterday, was beaded, his upper lip
pearled, the damp circles under his arms the size of garbage-can
lids and every bit as fragrant. Everybody overlooked it. This was,
after all, his birthday—Donny Harrison—and nobody wanted to
risk being rude . . . except of course Donny Harrison.

He was the boss.

He was the wonder guy behind Wonder Guy, the comic-book
sensation that had put Americana Comics on top back in '38.
Every kid in America would have recognized that costume with
its big white W sewn center-chest, although five-foot-eight, two-
hundred-eighty-pound Donny Harrison's physique hardly matched
their hero's, nor would their hero likely have a glass of bourbon in
one paw and a Cuban cigar in the other.

Wonder Guy—by day mild-mannered radio reporter Ron Benson—was a clean-cut superhuman from the planet Crylon. He could fly, he could bend steel with his bare hands, he could bounce the bad guys' bullets back at them just by sticking his chest out. Every boy in America (and quite a few men) harbored fantasies of being a real-life Wonder Guy.

But Donny had no such fantasies. In his mind, he was a true wonder guy—the small-time publisher/distributor of girlie mags who had slapped together a handful of rejected comic-strip samples as a cheap booklet that had, like Wonder Guy from a rooftop, taken off. That two kids from Des Moines, Iowa, had created Wonder Guy meant little to him. He was the visionary who published it, and whose wining and dining of regional wholesale distributors had made Wonder Guy a household name.

Watching Donny thread clumsily through the cocktail party— a mix of his friends and enemies from Americana Comics as well as assorted representatives of newspapers, magazines, local theaters and fashionable shops—was a study in absurdity. Not that the crowd was poshly attired—this was a late-afternoon fete attended mostly by business people before heading home. My tan tropical worsted and lighter tan shirt with blue-and-brown patterned tie was fairly typical, even if my brown rubber-soled moccasins were a fashion step nobody else in the room had taken.

And I was probably the only attendee not taking full advantage of the open bar. I was having rum and Coke, minus the rum. I'd been on the wagon for five years and had no intention of falling off on the occasion of Donny Harrison's fiftieth birthday.

This was Wednesday, late afternoon, in the suite of Donny's executive secretary, Harriet "Honey" Daily. She was the best-looking woman in the place, and perhaps it was no surprise she found her way through the blue fog of tobacco smoke over to the best-looking man, a six-footer with chiseled features, dark blue eyes and dark brown hair (easy on the hair tonic), drinking rum and Coke, minus the rum.

"It's too bad," she said.

She was a striking blonde in her midthirties, her hair shoulder-length but pulled back off her heart-shaped face to better frame the apple cheeks, big china blue eyes, perfect pug nose, full red-lipsticked lips and gently cleft chin. The coral crepe dress was simple but for the white scroll embroidery on her shoulders right up to the keyhole, bow-trimmed neckline. The lines of it didn't hide her curves but didn't shout about them, either.

"What's too bad?" I asked.

She sipped her martini. "That Donny's such an obnoxious drunk. He really can be quite charming, you know."

"I've managed to miss that, all these years."

She eyed me, the full lips pursing in a wry kiss. "And we've managed never to meet, somehow. But you're Jack Starr, all right."

"And you're Miss Daily."

"Honey."

"This is so sudden."

She laughed just a little; it was all my quip deserved. "No, I mean, please call me 'Honey.' All my friends do."

I glanced around at the little cliques in the spacious suite's living room, a modern study in coral and emerald leather furniture and all-glass tables on fluffy white carpet. A white baby grand in the adjacent dining room, over by a window on the city, was getting its ivories tinkled by a colored jazz pianist in a white dinner jacket who I recognized from the hotel's Blue Room. Cole Porter tunes, mostly.

"Do your friends," I asked lightly, making sure to attach a smile, "include Mrs. Harrison?"

Mrs. Harrison was indeed present, currently talking to her husband's business partner, Louis Cohn, vice president and chief accountant of the funny-book firm. Mrs. Harrison was a stout woman with a round pleasant face, almost pretty; but she had done herself no favor picking out that floral tent she was bivouacked in and her white hat looked like a bottle cap. She was holding a martini, stiffly, as if it might drink her, if she weren't so very careful.

Since Honey Daily was Donny Harrison's mistress—her title of executive secretary was essentially honorary, since nobody at Americana Comics had seen her at the office since that first six months in 1940 when she really had been Donny's secretary— you might think I'd get slapped for such a rude remark. Or maybe my hostess would just glare and storm away.

But Honey Dailey was if anything not predictable. She was one of these sophisticated women you hear so much about but rarely meet, even in Manhattan.

She said, "You've got cheek, Mr. Starr."

"You got your share of cheeks, too . . . Honey. And I'm not complaining."

She laughed gently. Sipped more martini. "Mrs. Harrison

chooses to accept the pretense that I'm her husband's secretary. Everyone else has quietly agreed not to make an issue of it."

Despite this being afternoon, the pianist was having at "Night and Day."

I arched an eyebrow. "But does Donny really have to rub his wife's face in it? I mean, even when she was your age, you could have made her look like a sofa."

"Especially in that dress," she said, with a smirk that should have made me hate her.

Instead I was thinking about her various cheeks again.

"What the hell," I said. "How many fiftieth birthdays does a guy get?"

Wonder Guy Donny was across the room, putting his arm around somebody else's wife and grinning in the poor woman's face.

Honey said, "Donny doesn't drink around me."

This seemed slightly out of nowhere. But I managed, "Oh really?"

Surely cocktail repartee, particularly with jazz pianists noodling Cole Porter in the background, should be sharper than "Oh really"; yet that's all I had.

But she didn't needle me. Just said, "He's a sweetheart, around home."

Apparently "home" was this coral-and-emerald suite at the Waldorf.

She turned the big light blue eyes on me and her eyelashes fluttered. I wondered for a moment if it was natural or an affection; then I decided I didn't care.

"I'd like to get to know you," she said.

"What would Donny say?"

"I'm not slipping the key to my suite in your pocket or anything."

"Damn."

That got a little laugh, more than it merited. "I've watched you . . ."

"From afar?"

One corner of her mouth turned up. "Something like that. It's just that . . . well, you're the topic of conversation, time to time."

I sipped my rum and Coke, minus the rum. "Am I now? Is it my good looks or my rapier wit?"

"They haven't come up, your looks and your wit."

"Ah."

I can do both "Oh" and "Ah," you see. For years I was on the short list for the Algonquin Round Table.

She traded her empty martini glass for a full one on a tray a uniformed Waldorf waitress was gliding by with. Across the room Donny was doing the same, except his other hand was on the waitress's rump.

"But I have noticed them," she said. And sipped. "Your good looks."

"And my wit."

"That, too." She cocked her head, looked around the room. "Where is your stepmother?"

"Not here, I'm afraid."

"Pity. I would have loved to meet her."

"I'm afraid she's at the office."

Her shrug was a little studied. "I would have thought she'd be here . . . that she'd be one of those flamboyant, bigger-than-life people. Filling up a room like this without even trying."

"Well," I admitted, "she would if she were here. But she's in one of her reclusive phases. Afraid I'm the sole emissary of the Starr Syndicate."

Honey frowned and managed not to produce any wrinkles, all eyes and mouth; impressive. "What do you mean, reclusive phase?"

"It's kind of personal."

"Personal for her, or you?"

". . . She's a little on the vain side. When she thinks she's too overweight to be seen in public, she hibernates."

"Oh my."

I'd said too much. I leaned closer. "Listen, she hasn't porked up or anything. She's probably twenty pounds over what she describes as her 'fighting weight,' and if she were here, she'd still be the best-looking woman in the room. Second best."

Honey didn't pursue that, but the baby blues had a twinkle when she asked, "Your father was in business with Donny, wasn't he?"

I nodded. "The major had a printing concern with both Donny and Louis. Started out together printing Yiddish newspapers and worked their way all the way up the ladder to racing forms and smut."

"Smut?"

"Well . . . sleaze, anyway. I wonder how many parents around the country know the publisher of *Wonder Guy Comics* started out shilling nudie pics of showgirls and strippers."

She studied me, her mouth amused but her eyes serious.

One of the cliques, over near the bar (predictably), was strictly
cartoonists—the creators of *Wonder Guy*, writer Harry Spiegel
and artist Moe Shulman, and artist Rod Krane, creator of the
other big Americana Comics success, Batwing, a sort of modern-
day Zorro with pointy ears.

Businesslike in a dark suit and dark blue tie, Harry was a little
guy with a pie-pan face, gesticulating and loud and laughing too
much; Moe was a head bigger, in a slept-in-looking brown suit
and brown tie, with a big oblong head and glasses so thick they
made his little eyes seem normal size. Krane was in between in
height but seemed to loom over both men, a confident, dark-eyed
guy with sharp, handsome features in a sharp, handsome dark
gray Brooks Brothers with black and gray tie on a gray shirt. He
was smoking a cigarette in a holder. Would I kid you?

We'd both been working on our drinks for a few seconds, just
lolling in the chatter and clink and smoke and jazzy piano, when
I swung my attention back to Honey because she had asked,
"Major?"

"Pardon?"

"You refer to your father as 'the major'?"

I laughed, once. "Yeah, well . . . we weren't real close. Everybody called Simon Starr the major. He was a major in the first
war, and a major character in life—made Donny look like a wall-
flower."

She laughed, once. "Well . . . he must have been a good-
looking man. Or did you get your looks from your mother?"

"He was short and fat. Mom was a showgirl. You can work
that out yourself."

Her smile had a warmth, now. "Do you mind another personal question?"

I shrugged. "Sure. I was first to get cheeky, wasn't I? Fire away."

"How many times was your father married?"

I held my fingers up in the Boy Scout salute. "Three. My mother died bringing me into the world. It's up to the world whether that was a fair trade."

"Oh, I'm sorry . . . ."

"It was twenty-eight years ago. I'm pretty well over it. I remember his second wife, vaguely. She was a star in George White's *Broadway Scandals of '37*. Then there was a Hollywood scandal in '39, when she and a married cowboy actor got roped in a motel by a divorce dick with a flash camera."

She said, "Oh, I'm sorry," again, but was laughing a little this time. "Was your . . . your mother a star?"

"No. She was in the *Follies* of '28 or '29 or something. Chorus gal—second from the end. Very pretty, though. I met her sister, my aunt—a housewife in Ohio. If my mother was like her, my dad did all right."

Honey had been building up to something. "Your father . . . the major . . . he married only showgirls, then."

"That's right. Same kind of talent he and Donny and Louie were putting in their *Spicy Models* magazine. Just seemed to be the circle he was moving in. Of course marrying Maggie Starr was moving up in the world."

Honey nodded. "She was a *real* star . . . even in the movies, wasn't she?"

"Maggie made a few flicks."

She cocked her head, RCA Victor doggie-style. "But I'm confused about something."

"I am here but to clarify."

"Wasn't her name *already* Starr when she married your father?"

"It was indeed. Her stage name, anyway. Her real last name is Spillman. But already having Starr on all her luggage and so on was a plus in the deal, I suppose."

She had finally gotten around to eating the olive off the toothpick in her latest martini. It was fun to watch.

Then she said, with a delicacy that was almost too much, "What's it like, having Maggie Starr for a stepmother?"

"I don't think of her that way," I said, truthfully.

"But she's . . . beautiful. Probably, next to Gypsy Rose Lee, the most famous . . . famous . . ."

"If you're trying to remember the polite word, it's ecdysiast. But regular joes like me just say stripper."

She shook her head and the blonde locks shimmered under the suite's subdued lighting. "That doesn't do her justice, does it? She spoofed striptease. Made a joke out of it."

"Yeah, but she still took her clothes off. Otherwise Minksy wouldn't've paid her."

The big blue eyes narrowed; the long lashes quivered as she thought about that. Then she asked, "She's stopped, hasn't she?"

"Yes. When she inherited the family business, that was the end of one kind of stripping . . . and the beginning of another."

Her laughter tinkled, counterpointing the piano player's tinkling of "I Get a Kick Out of You." "You mean, she syndicates comic strips."

"That's right. She still considers herself a stripper of sorts."

"She sounds wonderful."

"She can be."

"That sounds . . . guarded."

"Well . . . she is my boss."

The eyes narrowed again. "Why didn't your father put you in charge of the business?"

"Yeah, why didn't he? . . . I need to freshen my drink. Care to come along?"

She took my arm and accompanied me. We were halfway to the little portable bar the Waldorf had provided, along with a uniformed bartender, when Donny trundled up, his Wonder Guy costume soaking with sweat. He was between cigars and bourbons, for which small blessing I was grateful.

He grinned at me, his bulging features friendly but the hand he laid on my shoulder squeezing a little too hard. "You ain't trying to steal my private secretary, are ya, kid?"

"No, Donny. I was just getting to know her. We've never met. Somehow she was never around the office when I dropped by."

He just smiled at that, flashing his big fake choppers. My God, he was perspiring, even for Donny. Then he whispered in my shell-like ear.

"You're not up to something, are you, kid?"

"No."

"Don't mean with Honey, here. You're not that dumb. I mean with the boys."

He meant Harry Spiegel and Moe Shulman.

"I don't follow you, Donny."

17

"Don't you and Maggie get cute, is all I'm saying."

I turned to look at him, close enough to kiss him, which I chose not to. "Maggie's gorgeous and I'm a handsome devil. Cute doesn't come into it."

That made him laugh; his breath was everything tobacco and booze could accomplish in one mouth. He patted my cheek, a little too hard to be affectionate.

"Don't do anything I wouldn't do," he said with good-natured menace, and bounded off, cape flapping. He was heading toward the table with the big sheet cake and mints and nuts, like at a wedding. A spread of hors d'oeuvres was at another table in the dining room adjacent—Donny was feeling in a generous birthday mood.

At the bar I got a fresh glass of Coke on the rocks and Honey noticed I was more a Shirley Temple than martini kind of guy.

"You aren't on the job, are you?" she asked.

"What do you mean?"

"Well . . . my understanding is, you're kind of a troubleshooter for the Starr Syndicate."

"My official title is vice president."

A single eyebrow rose. "I was thinking of your duties. If there's a lawsuit, or if one of the cartoonists or columnists gets in a jam, don't you . . . step in?"

"You might say that."

Now both eyebrows hiked. Still no wrinkles. "Then you're not . . . an editor or anything."

I shrugged. "I offer an opinion, when asked."

"Are you asked?"

"Time to time. What are you getting at?"

"I don't know. I just noticed you were drinking, uh . . ."

"Rum and Coke, minus the rum?"

She smiled. She had lovely teeth. Much nicer than Donny's, even if he had paid top dollar for his. "I thought . . . I thought maybe Donny had . . . nothing. Sorry."

She hadn't heard any of what her charming part-time roommate had whispered to me.

"Oh," I said. "You thought Donny had asked my . . . stepmother to send me over as a sort of . . . bodyguard. Security person? Because of certain . . . tensions."

Tensions like Mrs. Harrison being present. Tensions like the storm brewing between Americana Comics and the team who created *Wonder Guy*.

"Something like that," she admitted.

"Nothing like that. That's not a gun in my pocket, I'm just glad to see you. It's just . . . I don't drink spirits."

"Oh."

"I used to."

". . . Oh."

"I majored in drinking in college and they flunked me out for doing such a good job. Then when I was in the service, I was in position to see, well . . . the results of overambitious drinking, let's say."

She cocked her head again. I liked the way her blonde locks fell when she did that. I liked the intelligence in those big light blue eyes, too. If I *had* been drinking spirits, I would have been in love with her by now, instead of only halfway there.

I answered her unposed question. "I was stateside, during the war. I was in the military police. I put a lot of drunk kids in the stockade. It . . . sobered me up."

"That's . . . that's admirable."

"Yeah, I was up for sainthood, till the Catholics found out about my heritage. Not that many Jewish saints."

She chuckled, then sipped. "I'm Jewish, too . . . nonpracticing."

"Yeah, I'm way out of practice, too. Listen, I don't have a secretary."

Her eyes got large and so did her smile. "You don't? A great big vice president like you?"

"No, I'm on the road a lot. Troubleshooting? And there's a secretarial pool at work I can dive into, when I want."

Her smile got kiss-puckery, again. "I bet you do."

"Anyway . . . if you ever, uh . . . need a new position . . ."

She grinned. "Well, doesn't *that* sound dirty."

"I didn't mean it to. It's the rum and Coke."

"Minus the rum."

"Yeah." I risked putting the tip of my finger under the cute cleft chin. "Anyway, if you should ever get tired of that fat bastard in the cape over there, give me a jingle."

Her smile was crooked now and she arched the other eyebrow—ambidextrous with brows, this one. "I happen to like that fat bastard in the cape."

"I'm sure you do. But I notice you said 'like.' That gives me hope."

And I toasted her with my glass, said excuse me and wandered over to the clique of cartoonists.

Harry Spiegel's dark, close-set eyes lighted up when I entered the artists' circle.

"Well, it's the Starr of the syndicate! Jackie boy, you look like a million dollars!" Harry gestured to me and grinned at his partner Moe, who smiled and nodded at me, a gentle smile, a gentle nod, while Rod Krane regarded me with his own smile, not so gentle, more on the suspicious side, or maybe it was the cigarette holder.

I put a hand on Harry's shoulder. "I hope you're not trying to butter me up, guys," I said to them both, ignoring Krane. "I don't make the decisions on new strips, you know."

The team behind *Wonder Guy* had submitted a new comic strip to the Starr Syndicate. I was fairly certain Maggie had decided to take it on, but it wasn't my place to say.

Krane, whose voice was resonant but edged with sarcasm, said, "She knows all about stripping, right, Jack?"

This was Krane's idea of wit. Try to imagine how many jokes I'd already heard about the famous striptease artist who now ran a comic-strip syndicate.

Harry frowned—he basically had two expressions, too happy and too irritated, and this was the latter. "Can you even stand it? Can you even stomach it?"

"I'll bite, Harry," I said. "Stand what? Stomach what?"

"That fat son of a bitch parading around in that Wonder Guy suit! It's a desecration of the costume. It's a travesty!"

Moe Shulman said, "Doesn't hurt anything."

His partner glared at him. "How can you say that? Wonder Guy stands for honesty, equity and the patriotic way!"

"I know, Harry," Moe said. The amplified eyes behind the thick glasses were glazed. And sad.

Krane said, "I think the co-creator of Wonder Guy knows what his character stands for, Harry. They say it at the start of every episode of the radio show, don't they?"

"For which we don't get a blessed cent!" Harry sputtered, spittle flying.

Other little groups of cocktail-party attendees were stealing glances at us.

I asked, "Harry, why did you come, if it upsets you?"

Harry's features were clenched like a fist. "Because it's the first time Donny Harrison ever deigned to invite us to one of his affairs! We were always second-class citizens . . . weren't we, Moe? Rod?"

Moe nodded. Krane shrugged and nodded; he was working on a martini, in between cigarette-in-holder puffs, looking like he stepped out of an *Esquire* fashion layout.

"He only invited us," Harry said, "to rub it in. This clown traipses all over the country, telling reporters and wholesalers and God and everybody that *he's* the guy behind *Wonder Guy!*"

Moe said, softly, "I don't think that's why we're here, Harry. For Donny to rub it in."

"Why, then?"

"I think this is Donny's idea of being nice to us. *He's* the one buttering us up, not Jack, here. Donny's the one that knows our ten-year contract'll be up soon, and then what?"

"Listen to Moe," Krane advised Harry, trading an empty glass for a fresh martini off a passing tray. "Three of us are gonna be in the cat-bird seat, before you know it."

Krane's ten-year contract was also about to expire.

The *Batwing* cartoonist was saying to his colleagues, "Donny wants to make nice, let him. Stay calm. Like the jazz cats say, don't lose your cool."

"I'm cool," Harry sputtered, "I'm cool."

I patted his shoulder. "Rod's right. You guys are still the talent behind the feature. With the new contract, you've got the perfect opportunity to feather your nests."

Harry brightened, like a kid who just heard about Christmas for the first time. "You think so, Jack? You really think so?"

"You bet."

That was when I noticed what Harry and Moe were drinking: beers. Everybody else had cocktails, but the creators of *Wonder Guy*, the makers of the feast, had made a workingman's, blue-collar choice.

I wandered over to pay my respects to Louis Cohn and Donny's wife, Selma. I knew Louis well—he was the only man here in a tuxedo and might have been taken for a head waiter, by the uninitiated—but had only met Selma a few times, most memorably ten years before at her and Donny's twentieth wedding anniversary party, also held here at the Waldorf. But not in Donny's mistress's digs.

"Mrs. Harrison," I said, nodding and smiling, "lovely to see you. Wonderful party."

"I'm Selma, Jack." Her voice was a musical alto touched by the remainder of a lower east side accent. "Surely we know each other well enough by now for first names."

We didn't, really, but that was fine by me.

She had very nice features; I had a feeling she'd been fetching, as a girl. Rounded out, she was a fairly typical housewife—right now, a housewife trying too hard, wearing a little too much makeup, her hair a nest of brown curls under the little white hat. Looking at her, I could have cried; or punched Donny for being such a lout, having his stupid party, here.

None of this had stopped me from half-loving Honey Daily, however; in the days to come, I'd find out just how many men had fallen for her.

But right now I was making small talk with Selma, asking about their two children, a daughter in junior high, a son in high school (neither present, thankfully).

Then, out of nowhere, she said, "I liked the major very much."

"My father? Well . . . thanks."

"Were you close?"

"Yes and no."

Louis Cohn—tall and dark and mustached, thinning hair combed back, looking severe in his tux and bow tie—said, "That's a hell of a thing to say, Jack. What do you mean?"

"We weren't close like some fathers and sons. He was gone a lot, on the road—you know what his business was like, Louie."

Cohn's chin went up defensively; he seemed to think we were arguing. "He built the Starr Syndicate from scratch."

I nodded. "He had a knack for the common man's tastes—when he picked up *Mug O'Malley*, every syndicate in the country had already turned it down."

Sam Fizer's *Mug O'Malley*, the boxing strip, was one of the nation's top features, fifteen years later.

Cohn was nodding now, not frowning, which was about as affable as he got. "Your father had an eye for talent."

And the ladies, but that was another story.

I said, "He made a point out of spending one week a year with me. For that week, we'd be close."

Selma, her dark blue eyes sparking with interest, asked, "What would you do?"

"All sorts of things. We tried hunting one year, fishing another—he wasn't an outdoorsman, and neither am I, so it was always a comedy of errors. But we had great fun together. Couple times, we spent a week going to one Broadway show after another. One year we went to Hollywood, and he used his contacts there to introduce me to all my favorite movie stars. Visited soundstages, got glossies hand-signed to me, the works. More than once we went to the World Series together. He was a great father."

One week a year.

"A whole week a year," Selma said wistfully. "That's a lot for a man like the major. That's a big gift he gave you. I hope you know it."

"Yeah," I said. "Sure."

"I miss the major," Louis said with absolutely no emotion.

Did he mean it? Or was that some kind of rote gesture?

Then he dropped a small bombshell. "Are the rumors about the boys true?"

The "boys" again—Spiegel and Shulman.

I managed not to sigh. "What rumors would those be, Louie?"

"That they've taken their new strip idea to you."

"You'd have to take that up with Maggie."

His hard eyes narrowed; his was a face full of creases. "Your stepmother hasn't been returning my calls."

"Well, she's been up to her famous backside in work, Louie. I'm sure she means no offense."

I knew Maggie was waiting to talk to Cohn until after we'd met with the "boys" ourselves, a meeting scheduled for tomorrow morning, actually.

"Tell your mother something, would you?" he asked, coldly polite. He had dark tiny eyes, like a shark. But that isn't fair . . .

. . . to a shark.

"What's that, Louie?"

"Ask her to check her toast tomorrow morning."

"Her toast?"

"Yes. Her toast. Ask her to check and see which side it's buttered on."

I didn't say anything. I just nodded to Mrs. Harrison and said, "Selma. Pleasure. Louie—always a treat."

I hit the john and cursed Louie Cohn while I pissed, and was heading back to the bar to work on refilling my bladder with another rum and Coke (you do the joke) when someone slipped her arm into mine.

Honey.

She beamed up at me, batted her lashes and asked, "Miss me?"

"I was wondering if that was heartburn or heartache."

"Like I'm wondering if you're a rat or not?"

"It'll come to you."

She squeezed my arm and pressed a breast against me, which

was the most fun I'd had in a couple of days. "Listen, Jack—Donny's going to cut the cake."

"Just so long as he doesn't cut the cheese."

"You're evil," she said, but she was laughing as she walked me along. We were clearly headed toward the table where the cake and mints and nuts (including Donny) awaited.

She was almost whispering. "I'd just like you at my side, is all."

I got it: I was the temporary beard. She wanted a front-row spot for Donny's birthday speech, and needed a male arm to hang on to that wasn't Donny's. That was fine. I'd always wanted to be used by a woman who looked like Honey Daily.

Sy Mortimer—a short, balding, pear-shaped fellow in a brown suit and a flapping *Wonder Guy* tie (the hero was in full flight)—was calling the meeting to order, clapping and yapping.

"Everybody! Everybody!" Sy was yelling. "Time for the man of the hour! Time for our wonderful Wonder Guy birthday boy to say something!"

Just behind and to the right of Sy, the sweat-drenched paunchy Wonder Guy was standing near the linen-covered table, with a big pointy knife in hand, ready to cut the huge sheet cake (white frosting trimmed with red and blue), which was garishly emblazoned with a stuck-on cut-out of Wonder Guy in flight with a frosting speech balloon saying HAPPY 50TH, DONNY! KEEP FLYING!

Sy—the recently appointed top editor at Americana, an ass-kisser of the first order—was clapping so insistently that everybody followed suit. The entire cocktail party had gathered around now, and the pianist was playing a jazzed-up version of the theme from the *Wonder Guy* radio show.

"Speech!" Sy called, and coaxed the audience, perhaps half of whom joined in. *"Speech!"*

Donny waved, knife in hand, at the crowd, for them to quiet down, which they were only too happy to do.

Then he spoke: "This is a happy day for me. Half a century, you believe it? . . . I see so many friends here . . . my lovely bride, Selma . . . ."

The most enthusiastic applause so far followed, and even Honey clapped politely, at my side, as Selma nodded around and smiled in acknowledgment.

"I been blessed to have business partners who was also my friends . . . I see young Jack Starr, there—your pop, the major, where would we all be without him?"

More applause. Nothing major.

"And Louie, who counts every penny—is that a rental tux, Lou?"

A little laughter.

"And we want our talented boys to know we appreciate what they done over the years—Moe, Harry, Rod. . . . "

Real applause. I glanced over and saw Harry beaming, bright as a beacon, but Moe looked glum and Krane smug.

Donny was weaving through all this speechifying. He looked, frankly, a little sick, pale around the gills. And that costume was sopping.

With his free hand he gestured, like a man trying to clear smoke, and with all the cigarettes and cigars in this room, there was some.

"I want you people to know I love you all . . . I love you all . . . . Wonder Guy himself never had it better."

That was when he started to totter—a collective gasp went up—and then his legs went out from under him like a wobbly card table folding up and suddenly he belly flopped onto the floor, with a crunch . . . right onto the hand clenching the knife.

I was the first one to him, and when I turned him over, it was the damnedest thing: the blade was stuck almost dead center in the W, jammed to the hilt from all that blubber hitting the white carpet so hard. Women were screaming, Honey and Mrs. Harrison included, and men, most of them Jewish, were yelling, "Jesus Christ!"

A gray-faced, silent Donny hadn't even had time to stop smiling. He was grinning up at the ceiling, or maybe the sky, as if Wonder Guy might be up there waving at him.

If so, he was waving good-bye.

I settled into the comfy wine-colored tufted leather chair across from Maggie Starr, president of the Starr Newspaper Syndication Company (Starr Syndicate for short).

Maggie's chair was tufted leather as well, and even more comfortable, but deep brown and swivelable behind a cherry desk smaller than a Buick, just. The desk was stacked with work, neat little obsessive piles—letters and comic-strip submissions and color proofs and columnist copy.

The office is a large narrow room with dark rich wood paneling, a very male bastion dating to when the major bought and remodeled the six-story brick building back in '32. The floor was parquet and mostly covered by a massive Oriental rug, with the left wall taken up by bookshelves still holding a leather-bound collection of classics the major bought but never cracked; the right wall displayed an array of framed posters of Maggie's Broadway revue, her three movies and two burlesque cards, one showing her billed above Abbott and Costello. The rear wall was wooden filing cabinets over which hung a dignified portrait of the major, framed in gilt. Various dark wood seat-upholstered chairs were lined against the walls, making it possible for a sizeable meeting to be held before Queen Maggie's throne.

Right now, next to me, were two of those chairs, awaiting our guests, Harry Spiegel and Moe Shulman. They were due in twenty minutes, at 10 A.M.

I'd filled Maggie in about Donny Harrison's memorable birthday party last night, over dinner, in the private room in the Strip Joint, the restaurant that takes up the first floor of the Starr Building.

I believe I mentioned the Strip Joint in passing, but you deserve more. When the major bought the building, a Chinese restaurant was in that space, and so it remained till Maggie ran across a fingernail in her eggroll, after which she refused to renew the lease, and put in her own restaurant (and hadn't eaten Chinese since). The chef she imported from a chophouse in St. Louis, but the layout and decor of the place was all her own doing.

When you come in off the street, the bar is at left and the barroom area takes up the front third of the long, narrow space. The front area is dark wood trim and glass and chrome, and the tan plaster walls are arrayed with signed framed photos of Maggie and her fellow (if "fellow" is the word) strippers. The barmaids wear white shirts with black tuxedo ties and black tuxedo pants and, often, the same faces as certain of the girls in the framed pics. Since stripping was still illegal in New York—part of Mayor La

Guardia's lasting legacy—Maggie provided work for retired Manhattanite striptease artists, as well as currently practicing ecdysiasts, when they were between gigs on the road.

The rear two-thirds of the space was given over to the restaurant, wooden booths and linen-covered tables, and the walls were white but covered with cartoons drawn right on the painted plaster. Maggie's grand opening, in '42, had been cartoonists only, the night before the National Cartoonists Society had their annual dinner; so not only had the Starr Syndicate talent drawn their famous characters on the walls, so had King Features luminaries like Alex Raymond and his *Flash Gordon* and Chic Young and *Blondie*, and the Tribune Syndicate's Chester Gould with *Dick Tracy* and Harold Gray with *Little Orphan Annie*, and even NEA's V. T. Hamlin (*Alley Oop*) and Roy Crane (*Captain Easy*).

So the Strip Joint served up both brands of strippers, the burlesque kind and the funny-paper variety, not to mention its famed strip steak. Lunch attracted businessmen who enjoyed being fussed over by pretty (if fully clothed) peelers; and supper, early and late, brought in a largely out-of-town crowd, particularly with the theater scene so nearby.

Even so, the restaurant business is rough, and I suspect Maggie kept the Strip Joint going so she didn't have to either hire a live-in cook or sling a pot or pan herself. When she was at her fighting weight (118), she might doll up and mingle with the guests and take a table out with the public, signing autographs and flirting with the men and telling the women how stunning they looked and pointing out Popeye and Nancy and Wonder Guy on the walls to the kiddies.

But when she was in her reclusive mode, Maggie had her meals sent up on trays, which she ate either in her office or up in her top-floor living quarters. Occasionally she ate in a small private room in the restaurant—designed to accommodate a single table for no more than six—when she had a guest or when she needed to talk business over a meal with one of her minions. Like me.

I guess while I'm at it I should give you the full layout. Street level is the restaurant. What we call the first floor is the editorial offices of the syndicate, the second floor is sales and distribution, the third is my apartment, the fourth is a reception area, Maggie's office and her personal gym, the fifth is her suite of rooms. These are all laid out boxcar-style, with a street entrance separate from the restaurant and a postage-stamp entry with an elevator including uniformed operator, eight to six, door locked otherwise.

So in that private Strip Joint alcove last night, over a bowl of potato soup (Donny dying took a bite out of my appetite), I'd filled Maggie in on the birthday party. She was eating a meal consisting strictly of salad with lots of rabbit food in it and vinegar and oil dressing. She was doing this because she was "huge" (my guess: 135 pounds). She hadn't said much, except, "The major loved Donny. I never understood why."

Mostly I reported everything I'd witnessed and everyone I'd seen there, not detailing my flirtation with Honey Daily. I have a near-photographic memory, although Maggie has on occasion accused me of having a pornographic memory instead, which is partly why I left out having developed a real rapport with the late birthday honoree's mistress.

But that was last night.

This morning, she'd clearly been giving Donny's demise some thought. At least, she was plainly troubled by something other than her excess seventeen pounds. She was leaning back in the chair, rocking gently, her long tapering fingertips (no nail polish but well-groomed long nails) tented, her face taut with thought.

Even sitting down, Maggie Starr looked tall—she was five-nine, after all—but the point was made by the huge, elaborately framed full-length portrait of her (in a form-fitting outfit of pink feathers) that hung right behind her. It dated to her 1941 Broadway revue, *Starr in Garter*, a gigantic pastel by Rolf Armstrong. Whether commissioned by the show's producer or Maggie herself, I never asked.

If you're thinking Maggie had a hell of an ego, you're right; but she mostly seemed to view the looming portrait as a reminder of what she was supposed to look like—like a woman hanging a new dress a size smaller than she is on a hanger on the refrigerator. I would see her steal glances up at the thing, and her expression would be as sour as a bitter-lemon cough drop.

Something else we should get out of the way: she was in fact my stepmother. She didn't give birth to me but she did use to sleep with the major, and that disquieting but undeniable reality cancelled out for me the fact that she was a stunning beauty. Anyway, she was older than me. She'd be forty before I was thirty.

Now you might be so tactless as to point out that just the afternoon before I'd had no trouble at all falling half in love with Honey Daily, who was thirty-five easy. But Honey Daily, to my knowledge anyway, never slept with my father. That I could get past her sleeping with a fat loathsome creature like Donny Harrison (RIP) will just have to remain one of the great enigmas of western civilization that we'll never solve.

Still, Maggie was, as I've said, stunning—even in her recluse-state wardrobe—pale-green scarf over her Lucille Ball hair, the faintest dab of lipstick on her trademark bee-stung lips, her big green eyes unaided by mascara, her pale, faintly freckled oval face as perfect as a carved cameo, her slender if bosomy figure hiding out under a green-plaid lumberjack shirt, sleeves rolled to her elbow. She'd been seated when I got there, but I would've bet a month's pay those long legs were on the lam under baggy blue denims.

Displaying that other trademark of hers—the deep, almost mannish voice coming out of a little-girl puss—she interrupted her troubled reverie to ask, "Too early for a Coke?"

She knew I despised coffee.

"Never," I said.

She pressed a small red button on her desk and shook her head. "Your poor teeth."

"My teeth are fine. All mine and nary a filling."

"The major lost his teeth before he was your age."

"Well, maybe my mother had nice teeth."

A little smile twitched. "Maybe she did. Before my time."

Her assistant Bryce (Maggie did not care for the term "secretary"—nor did Bryce) came briskly in behind me from his reception area-cum-office with tucked-away kitchenette. I liked Bryce, who was funny and smart and (to use the most current term) "gay." An alarmingly handsome, trimly bearded brown-eyed boy about twenty-five, he wore a black turtleneck sweater and black slacks but white rubber-sole shoes—I never asked.

He had been a dancer in Maggie's Broadway show during the run of which he'd broken an ankle, ending one career and picking up on another, which was to be chauffeur, secretary and whatever else Maggie might need on a whim. Sort of like that African giant in the leopard skin who follows Mandrake the Magician around.

Bryce had an apartment in the basement, below the restaurant, a rather dank little chamber for such a neat little character to live in. I wasn't sure I knew what went on down there but was positive I didn't want to.

Using a tray, Bryce delivered Maggie's coffee, so cream-laden it was damn near white, and provided me a Coca-Cola on ice.

He hovered over me like a guilty conscience and raised an accusing eyebrow. "What can we do to get her out of that babushka? Is she expecting a stiff wind?"

"That's not my department," I said.

"Will you tell her she looks fine. She needs to get out and about."

I looked at Maggie. "You look fine. Why don't you get out and about?"

"Mind your own business," she said, the target of her remark ambiguous.

When I looked back up at him, Bryce was still looming; he'd arched the other eyebrow in the meantime. "Will you tell her there's nothing wrong with a woman having a little meat on her bones. Will you tell her that men like women with curves? That people haven't paid good money for all these years to look at her goddamn rib cage?"

Maggie said, "What would you know about what men like? . . . Scratch that."

With a smile of unmatched superiority, Bryce and his tray took their leave.

"She has her nerve," I said.

"Don't be mean." Maggie sipped her coffee, reacting as if a much-needed blood transfusion had been provided her. "You know you like Bryce."

"I do. And you should listen to him."

Maggie sighed and unknotted the scarf, revealing a perfectly fine short-shorn tangle of natural curls—albeit of a shade of red unknown in nature—and stuffed it in a desk drawer. ". . . Any further comments about Donny's birthday party?"

"Let's just say I've heard of falling on your sword, but this is ridiculous."

She hiked an eyebrow—she had perfect dark naturally arching ones, requiring little if any plucking (she's told me so). "Yes. I hardly think it was suicide. Heart attack, I suppose."

"Well, we'll know, soon enough."

"We will?"

I nodded. "I overheard Mrs. Harrison talking to Louis Cohn—after the medics came and carted Wonder Guy away? She said her husband was in perfect health and she was going to know how in heaven's name this terrible thing could have happened to such a lovely man."

Maggie was nodding, and not at the notion Donny was a lovely man. "Which you take to mean she'll have an autopsy performed."

"Either that or buy herself a Ouija board. I'm gonna go with autopsy."

She was thinking. Like Honey Daily, she had perfected the art of reflecting without furrowing. "Donny Harrison was a lot of things, but in perfect health wasn't one of them."

"He was fatter than Andy Devine and smoked more than Groucho and drank more than Bogart. They should sell his liver to the Stage Door deli—it's bound to be pickled enough."

Maggie smiled but said, "Don't be disrespectful. Your father loved the man."

"You said that last night. His mistress—Honey Daily? She said he was simply charming at home." I was just about to ponder aloud why a dish like that would hook up with a fat lout like Donny when I remembered Maggie had married the major.

"You told me last night who was at the party," Maggie said. "But were there any conspicuous absentees?"

I thought about that, wondering what she was getting at. "Well, Harry Spiegel's wife wasn't there, I hear. Rose has never made a great secret of her contempt for the Americana brass, so maybe Harry leaving her home was the better part of valor."

"What about certain . . . silent partners?"

Now I got it.

I shook my head. "No sign of Frank Calabria or any of his delightful crowd."

"Well . . . you said there were press people present. That makes sense."

"Even if Frank does have his own suite at the Waldorf."

Maggie's upper lip curled. "You mean, *his* mistress has a tower suite, too. Mr. Calabria and his wife and children live on Central Park West."

"Oh, yeah, I forgot. He just stops by the Waldorf every day for his shave."

Frank Calabria was thought by those in the know to be the number one mobster in New York. And he had been a silent partner throughout the '20s and '30s in various business enterprises involving Harrison, Cohn and the major. All started back in Prohibition days, when publisher Harrison decided to buy his paper in Canada, for some reason. Think about it.

"You know," I said, "before he did the world a favor, Donny threatened me about us taking on Harry and Moe's new strip."

"Really." She sat forward, elbows on the desk, hands clasped. "You mentioned Louis Cohn . . ."

"Another of my father's really swell associates."

"He called this morning."

"About Donny's farewell party?"

"No. Which is just like Louis. Not a word of that until I brought it up halfway through the conversation." She sighed heavily and the breasts under the plaid made their whereabouts known. "He was calling about the same subject."

"What same subject?"

"What Donny threatened you over—telling us not to 'humor' the 'boys' on their new strip."

Now it was my turn to sigh. "Yeah, I forgot to tell you last night—Louie told me to remind you which side of the bread the butter goes on."

She shook her head. "I used to hear that saying as a kid in Council Bluffs. I never understood it."

"Yeah, well, I think Louie's meaning is pretty clear. Does he have any contractual right to screw with us?"

She shook her head. "You know as well as I the major made a clean break with Americana, years ago. Of course, I have a few shares of stock. And we have a first look at comic-strip syndication rights on any new comic-book feature they come up with."

"Tell you the truth, none of their strips are doing that hot for us."

We ran three strips derived from Americana comic books: *Wonder Guy*, *Batwing* and *Amazonia*, the latter basically a female version of Wonder Guy melded with the venerable woman warrior legend of the amazons. *Wonder Guy* still held a good list, though we'd lost maybe 20 percent of our papers, postwar. *Batwing* never had a huge list, despite the size of Rod Krane's ego, but was holding on and had its share of major cities. *Amazonia* looked to be gone in a year or two—a respectable list at the outset that was getting whittled away at every month.

"The bloom's definitely off the superhero rose," I said.

She was sipping her coffee. "Yes, but we have the two biggest stars in *Wonder Guy* and *Batwing*."

"I don't know—on the newsstands, comic-book market in general? *Marvel Man*'s outselling *Wonder Guy*, these days."

She nodded. "Yes, and I wish we could take out a strip version of that—nice light touch that appeals to kids *and* parents—but Cohn would foam at the mouth, if we did."

I had a sip of Coke. "Anyway, rumor is Cohn's planning to sue Spiggot Publications for plagiarism over *Marvel Man*. We don't need to be in the middle of that."

"We certainly do not." She sorted through some artwork on her desk. "But do we need *this?*"

I rose to take the samples of the new Spiegel and Shulman strip, *Funny Guy*. I'd seen them before but Maggie seemed to want me to have a second look.

Back in the leather chair, I flipped through the large comic-strip originals—like many cartoonists, Shulman worked "twice up," double the size of the printed version. The originals were beauties in their quirky way—on Crafttint, a chemically treated board that allows the artist to use a brush to bring up tones of shading in black-and-white art.

"Very professional," I said. "Looks like Moe's getting some help on the art."

"I think he *has* to."

I glanced up. "Oh?"

Maggie shrugged. "You've noticed those glasses of his."

I nodded. "Every time I see him, they seem even thicker."

Then she waved it off. "But that doesn't bother me. What cartoonist doesn't use assistants and ghosts?"

Six daily strips and a Sunday page, every damn week, is a heavy workload, a murderous grind, and Maggie was right about even the most dedicated workhorses among comic-strip artists needing a hand.

And to produce *Wonder Guy* for both the comic strips and monthly books, Spiegel and Shulman had had to assemble a studio of helpers, originally back in Iowa, the last few years here in New York. One bone of contention between the team and Americana was the comic-book company hiring other artists and writers to supplement the work coming from the creators and their studio.

"Sales tells me we can start with a strong list," she said, "but I doubt it'll hold up. The concept doesn't . . . well, let's just say I wouldn't consider this for Starr if it wasn't from a name brand like Spiegel and Shulman."

Funny Guy was an odd duck of a strip, no getting away from it—circus acrobat Sammy Laff would fight crime dressed up as the clownish, big-nose, big-shoes Funny Guy, spritzing tear gas from lapel flowers and surprising villains with exploding-cigar grenades, driving his Fun-Mobile and staging elaborate pranks.

I handed the strips back. "Does kind of try too hard."

Bryce stuck his head in the office. "I have Mr. Spiegel and Mr. Shulman for you, Miss Starr."

Always "Miss Starr," never "Mrs."

"Show them in," she said.

Harry Spiegel—spiffy in a tan sportscoat with padded shoulders and patch pockets over a green-and-white sportshirt with sporty brown trousers—came in first, of course, rushing over to shake hands with Maggie, who rose for the occasion, and then with me, grinning like Funny Guy himself. Moe Shulman, in that same slept-in-looking brown suit he'd worn yesterday, but with a blue sportshirt underneath, lumbered in after; he was smiling a little but seemed vaguely embarrassed about it. He just nodded at Maggie, politely, and shook my hand, with considerably less force than Wonder Guy might have.

Harry took the center chair and sat forward, while Moe slouched into his.

Bryce followed quickly behind them with a tray of iced teas, having already taken their order. Bryce set the tall, sweating, lemon-slice-sporting glasses on coasters on Maggie's massive desk nearby; my glass of Coke was on a similar coaster. Moe thanked Maggie's assistant, who nodded, but Harry hadn't seemed to notice the inconspicuous figure in full beard, black attire and white shoes.

"Beautiful day out there, Maggie," Harry said, beaming at her. "You really need to get out in that sunshine."

"I don't have the skin for it," she said with a gentle smile.

I said, "I see you're over Donny's death."

Harry turned to me and his face went blister white. "God, I don't mean to be a ghoul about it . . . . I mean, like the philosopher said, every man's death is every man's loss . . . or something."

"Or something," I said.

Maggie said, "A lot of people loved Donny Harrison—he put Americana on the map with his, well, his glad-handing and kick-backs and what have you. But I fully understand that finding any grief for him is a tall order for you and Moe."

If he'd sat any further on the edge of the chair, Harry would have been on the floor; his voice had something pleading in it as he said to Maggie, "I really don't mean to be a louse about this . . . but somehow, it's like . . . like a sign."

Maggie's eyebrows hiked. "A sign?"

"Of our new beginning. I mean . . . the sun *is* shining Everything is going great."

"Including having Donny fall on his birthday-cake knife," I said.

Harry managed to glare at me and yet at the same time seem like he might bust out crying, which I had a feeling he hadn't done yet, where the tragic loss of his publisher was concerned.

"Jack," he said, and it was almost a whine, "you make me sound terrible. I don't mean to gloat, really I don't . . . but Donny stabbed Moe and me in the back, over and over. He and Louie Cohn stole and cheated and lied . . . Jack, Maggie—*you* know the story."

We did—Harrison had paid $130 for the boys to turn their rejected *Wonder Guy* comic-strip samples into a cut-and-paste comic-book story. Buying all rights, as was typical at the time, and even now. He and Cohn had hired the boys to write and draw their own creation, paying them ten bucks a page.

Maggie was nodding. "But you have an industry-standard deal on the comic-strip version—fifty percent for you with the Starr Syndicate paying off Americana from our half. That's one of the best contracts in the business."

Harry's grin split his face. "That's because you and Jack here are salt of the earth. You're a kid from Iowa like Moe and me, Maggie, and you don't try to swindle and screw the talent. You're not out to steal our dreams! That's why we're back to do business with you again."

"But remember," she said gently, "Americana blessed the Starr Syndicate contract—Donny and Louis tried to do right by you, in that instance at least."

Finally Moe spoke up. "Yes, but you don't know about the toys and the candy and the movies and the radio show."

Maggie shrugged a little. "Admittedly, I don't. That's not any of my business."

With the expression of a man taking in skunk, Harry said, "They set up a whole separate company for that. A Wonder Guy company that handles licensing and we don't get a cent of it. They don't even say our names on the radio show. Americana made a real killing off of our character, and we got zippo! Zilch, zally! Greedy bastards, Maggie. Horrible people. The kind of people Wonder Guy punches out or puts in jail."

That was their problem, the boys. They were naive kids from Iowa who grew up on science-fiction magazines and hung around with other geeky unpopular kids and believed in the red-white-and-blue simplicity of pulp fiction and Hollywood morality plays. They were unprepared for a world where comic books featuring Wonder Guy punching out mobsters were financed in part by the likes of Frank Calabria.

But I didn't go into that, and neither did Maggie. Spiegel and Shulman were purveyors of an unsophisticated version of America to kids of all ages, arrested-development creators who were themselves incapable of understanding the more complicated underbelly of not just the business they were in, but existence on the planet Earth itself.

As opposed to the planet Crylon.

"Let's talk about *Funny Guy*," Maggie said.

"Let's!" Harry said brightly.

"You said Americana turned the property down."

"Yes. Sy Mortimer rejected it outright, but then, when I pressed him, admitted Donny and Louis had put their personal kibosh on it—said we already had *enough* on our plates with *Wonder Guy*!"

"Do you?" Maggie asked, lifting her eyebrows again; God, how did she do that without wrinkling her forehead? Amazing.

"Maggie," Harry said, "I'm one of the fastest writers in the business. Turning out scripts is no problem. Pages just fly out of my machine, like Wonder Guy up in the sky. And Moe's got a great bunch of youngsters helping him out."

Maggie had a thoughtful sip of coffee, then turned to his partner. "How much of the work are you able to do yourself, Moe?"

Moe, who was sipping coffee himself, frowned just a little—he'd picked up on that phrase: *Are you able to?*

"I design all the characters," he said, stiffly dignified, "and I do all the pencil layouts. And I ink the faces myself."

I said, "Pretty standard. Probably more than Sam Fizer's doing on *Mug O'Malley*."

Harry nodded vigorously but Moe just looked at me.

Maggie gestured to the sample strips and cocked her head as she said, "Very professional work. We *are* interested. Have you placed it elsewhere, as a comic book?"

"Oh yes," Harry said, bright-eyed. And bushy-tailed, goddamnit. "Comic Book Enterprises—one of Donny and Louie's former editors runs it—have committed to six issues. Our names are *big* on the cover! We can coordinate the launch of the strip with the comic."

"Good," she said. "Is doing the property somewhere other than Americana a problem? I mean . . . I don't mean to pry, but we're all aware your contract comes due soon, on producing

Wonder Guy comic books. And our arrangement with Americana on the strip version comes due only a few months after that."

I said, "You fellas are aware, aren't you, that Americana has the right, by contract, to specify who we use as artist and writer on the strip?"

Harry's face fell. "You wouldn't sell us out, would you?"

I shook my head, firmly. "Not a matter of selling you out. They can make us do it."

Harry batted the air. "Don't worry about it. We'll be fine. Zelly's on top of it."

Zelly was Bert Zelman, the team's lawyer, a smart hustler whose shingle had only been hung out a year ago. Harry had met Zelman when they were in the service together, Harry having served two years stateside as a company clerk, still turning out *Wonder Guy* scripts in his off-duty time. Moe had been 4-f— five'll get you ten, for his weak eyesight . . . .

I said, "If you boys actually did sell all rights, at the start of this shindig, couldn't you get fired? What I mean is, we at Starr don't want to be part of a disaster for you . . . giving you a home for *Funny Guy* and making you lose *Wonder Guy*."

Harry had already started shaking his head halfway through that. "Jack, Jackie boy—we got them by the short and curlies . . . excuse me, Maggie, didn't mean to be crude."

"I'll get over it," she said lightly.

"But Donny and Louie made a big blunder," Harry said, that face-splitting grin going again. "See, a few years ago, Moe and me submitted an idea for a spin-off feature—*Wonder Boy*. All about Wonder Guy's years growing up as a fun-loving kid, a small-town prankster learning to harness his powers for good. Well, they flat-out rejected it—Donny and Louie said, stick to the grown-up version. Nobody's gonna wanna see a kid version. Is exactly what they said. And in writing!"

I nodded, sipped Coke again. Maggie was just listening, fingertips tented.

Moe said, "And then a few months ago, they launched *Wonder Boy* as lead feature in *Exploits*. Without telling us. Without negotiating anything."

"Lousy thieves!" Harry blurted.

Now Maggie was nodding. "And it's a separate property. You may be right, fellas. They fouled up—they may well have opened the front door of the house."

"Meaning," I said, "in your contract renewal negotiations, you may get to rearrange all the furniture."

"Yeah!" Harry said, his smile huge and happy.

"Yes," Moe said, his smile small and sad.

"But, guys," I began, sitting forward, "why *Funny Guy*? If you're going to get *Wonder Guy* back . . . ."

"We just want to branch out a little," Harry said. "You know—explore our wealth of creativity."

But Moe cut through the BS. "Frankly, Miss Starr . . . Mr. Starr . . . we need to hedge our bets."

"You get tied up in court," I said, with a nod, "or things go badly, you'll need work. And cash flow."

Harry said, "I don't think of it that way."

But Moe admitted he did, saying, "Can't have all our eggs in one basket."

Harry shot Moe a nasty look, which was rare between them; they really were friends since high school. In Iowa. Christ.

From behind us came Bryce's voice in the doorway. "Miss Starr? . . . Sorry, I know you said no interruptions. But I have a Captain Chandler on the line."

"Captain of what?" Maggie asked, mildly irritated.

"The police, I suppose," Bryce said, with a grandiose gesture. "Isn't that what he meant when he said, 'Homicide'?"

The heat was enough to make me wonder if I looked wilted in my single-breasted tropical worsted, which was blue; my tie was bluer, with cheerful brown birds painted on—they had a right to be happy, they couldn't feel the heat—against a Sanforized blue-and-white-striped cotton shirt. But only a lingering sense of style and a dab of dignity kept me from running out into the spray of the fire hydrant that was blasting half a dozen kids in swim trunks, urchins splashing and dancing around out on the pavement in front of the Tenth Precinct Station House at 230 West Twentieth Street.

The Tenth Precinct's home lacked both style and dignity, a dingy six-story gray stone building fronted by three prominent arches framing a window, the entrance and a garage. Up two little steps and I was into the high-ceilinged reception area, decently cooled by overhead churning fans. At left was the receiving sergeant behind his judge's-bench-like desk, where I stopped for directions.

The sarge didn't even look up, just pointed over at the stairs where a painted sign with an upward-slanting arrow said HOMI-CIDE BUREAU, 3RD FLOOR. The stairs were creaky and the two flights stuffy, but soon I was through a door and under another whirring ceiling fan, trying to talk myself into thinking I was as cool as those kids out in the fire hydrant spray.

This medium-sized room was home to a reception desk and a small bullpen of four more desks for detectives (unmanned at the moment), as well as the expected pale green plaster walls, wire wastebaskets, hat rack, wooden benches, chairs and mismatched filing cabinets. Nothing about the dreary, institutional chamber built my confidence that the solving of Manhattan's many murders was in good hands.

The receptionist, a severe woman in her forties in a white short-sleeved blouse and glasses and a black ribbony thing at her throat, was expecting me; or anyway Captain Chandler was, and I only sat on a wooden bench for five minutes before being summoned to enter through the wood-and-frosted-glass door reading CAPTAIN. Another door read COMMANDING OFFICER, so I was not at the top of the ladder; but in New York police department terms, captain's up quite a few rungs.

Interestingly, Chandler had offered to come over to the Starr Syndicate personally, which raised all sorts of questions, complete with troubling potential answers.

I hadn't actually talked to the captain, Bryce having been in full protective intermediary mode; but when Maggie's assistant

conveyed the captain's desire to talk specifically to one Jack Starr
and could he come over to our offices to do so, she said crisply to
Bryce, "No," then to me, "*You* go to *him*."

In her reclusive phase, Maggie sees as few of her fellow human
beings as possible.

So at 2 P.M., give or take, I was inside Captain Chandler's private domain, a dreary office with a few wooden files, a bench
against a wall, a window onto the city to my left as I entered, a
window on a neighboring brick wall to my right. Under that window, where wainscoting met plaster, nails on the wooden trim
held various well-thumbed manuals and directories on metal
loops. The light green walls otherwise held scant decoration—a
framed police department seal, a framed picture of a graduating
class at the academy and assorted cracks and water stains.

Chandler's desk, big and dark brown and beat-up, was in the
middle of the room, putting the brick wall at his back, as well as
a corner-positioned two-drawer file atop which were two framed
photos (a pretty blonde wife posing alone and then with a boy
and girl of grade-school age), a pipe rack and a coffee mug with
CAPTAIN on it. Just in front of the file was a hat rack with one
lonely brown fedora.

My lonely fedora, dark blue, was in my hands as I stood and
waited for Chandler to get off the phone. He hadn't seemed to notice me yet.

He was maybe thirty and, if his legs weren't sawed off, my guess
was he was in the six-foot range, a broad-shouldered guy in rolled-
up white shirtsleeves and red-and-blue striped tie. He was handsome enough to hate—brownish-blond hair, dark eyebrows over

light blue eyes, strong cleft chin and an easy smile; if Hollywood had been casting him, he'd have been wrong for the part, unless the homicide cop was the star of the picture.

The ceiling fan was going full throttle, ruffling his hair, and he had various objects—coffee cup, box of .45 ammunition, handcuffs—weighting down stacks of fluttering papers on the desk; his two telephones were positioned to hold down other stacks. He was just finishing up on one of those phones—apparently talking to a pathologist—when he finally glanced up at me, flashed that smile and motioned me toward the waiting chair.

He hung up, stood and held out his hand. "Pat Chandler," he said, proving he was six foot. "Thanks for coming, Mr. Starr."

We shook hands, firm but not trying to impress each other.

Sitting, I said, "You didn't tell Miss Starr's assistant what the purpose of the visit was. He said you were a little . . . coy."

"Well, so was he," Chandler said, and laughed. Then he frowned a little: "Miss Starr? Isn't it *Mrs.* Starr?"

"Well, she's still in show business. She retains her theatrical maidenhood."

He was rocking in his swivel chair, chuckling to himself; the blue eyes seemed distant. "You know, your . . . she's your step-mother, right?"

"Yes. And my boss."

He twitched an embarrassed half smile. "Have to admit one of her pinups was plastered in every barracks and foxhole I ever found myself in. I was in the Pacific Theater."

"She's played plenty of theaters."

His eyes narrowed, but his expression remained friendly, and he continued to rock. "You were in the service, too, I understand. Army?"

"Yes."

He thumbed his chest. "Marines."

I shrugged. "Takes all kinds. Anyway. What was it you were going to—"

"You won the Silver Star."

Not this.

"Uh, yes, I did."

The eyes in that casual expression were studying me. "But I'm told you were stateside. How do you win a Silver Star stateside? I was on Guadalcanal and all I managed was a Purple Heart and a Ruptured Duck."

The Ruptured Duck was the Honorable Service lapel button everybody got who served.

"Gee, Captain Chandler," I said through a smile considerably less charming than the ones he was tossing around, "maybe you should've tried harder."

Finally I'd said something that didn't make him smile.

"I meant no offense," he said. He'd stopped rocking. "I just heard you got the Silver, and were stateside. You can't win a Silver Star without engaging enemy combatants, right? I just couldn't put one and one together and come up with two."

"Well, mine was the only stateside Silver Star, if you must know."

He raised a hand. "Again—no offense meant . . ."

"I was an MP."

He nodded. "That much I knew. So *you* were a cop, too."

"Yeah. You could say that."

Still trying to understand, shaking his head a little in mild confusion, he asked, "Where were you stationed?"

"Couple of places. In '45 I was one of sixty-four MPs watching a POW camp."

"In America?"

"Oklahoma—you know, like the Broadway show. We had fourteen hundred supermen who decided to break out one night. And things happened, and I got the Silver Star. It's not something I'm particularly proud of, and—"

"Not *proud* of! Jesus, man, you should be—"

"How much do you talk about Guadalcanal, Captain?"

That stopped him; his face whitened and he said, "Sorry. I get your point. I didn't mean to pry."

"Yeah, but, well, you kinda did, didn't you?"

He flashed the grin. "Hey, I'm a paid professional snoop. Allow me to thank you for keeping the Nazis out of the Bronx, and away from my wife and kids."

His grin, goddamnit, was working on me; so I grinned, too, and said, "Glad to. Now, what in the hell is so important that you were willing to hoof it over to our offices?"

He had all kinds of smile and grins, and this one was shy and self-effacing. "I just wanted to meet Maggie Starr, is all. Her picture got me through a lot of rough nights."

"Well, spare me any details you wouldn't also want to share with your wife and kids."

Now the grin cut itself in half and dug a dimple in one cheek.

"I understand you're the VP at the Starr Syndicate . . . what does the vice president of a comic-strip syndicate do?"

"Whatever the president asks him to."

He flipped at the edges of one of the stacks of weighted-down papers. "I mean, I ask because . . . frankly, Jack, I did a little checking on you."

"I'd be disappointed if you hadn't."

"And it turns out you're a licensed private investigator. Why is that, Jack? Why does the vice president of a comic-strip syndicate need to carry a private-eye ticket?"

I scratched my head, where my hair was getting riffled by the overhead fan blades. "Actually, we also syndicate crossword puzzles, and recipes, and a bridge column, several gossip—"

"Why, Jack?"

I sighed. "Captain, I sometimes have to protect our talent from everything from lawsuits to death threats. That license allows me to poke around, sometimes working with our attorneys, in areas a private citizen could not."

"So you're a licensed private investigator with one client."

"That's right—the Starr Syndicate. So if you want to have somebody check up on whether your brother-in-law is cheating on your sister, better have one of your dicks do that in his spare time."

He didn't waste a smile on that one. He just went to another of the piles of papers and tapped the top sheet with a finger. "Listen, I looked over your statement, taken by the officers at the Waldorf the other night."

The chair squeaked in protest as I shifted my weight in it. "So that's what this is about—Donny Harrison's death."

"Yes."

I shrugged. "Well, I didn't give a statement, exactly. Certainly not a full one. I don't suppose anybody did. There were four officers talking to sixty-some people, all of whom didn't want to be at that party anymore, especially with the bar shut down. So if you have further questions, I'm glad to accommodate. But I fail to see why the Homicide Bureau would be looking into an accident, even a bizarre one like this."

No smile; no grin. "When you were an MP, didn't you look into suspicious deaths?"

"Half a dozen times or more, sure. It was a long war. But what's suspicious about a fat sweaty bastard passing out and falling on something sharp? In front of umpteen witnesses?"

He also had a sizeable supply of frowns and showed me one of those. "You didn't like Donny Harrison?"

"He was one of my late father's best friends, and yet the thing I remember the major . . . my father . . . saying about Harrison, most often? Was that he was a first-class genuine horse's patoot."

His face had settled into a professional blankness, but the eyes were sharp. "But you did business with him."

"Not much. We syndicate three comic strips to newspapers, all across this great land, that are licensed to us by Americana Comics. Donny Harrison and Louis Cohn, the two principle stockholders in the company, the publisher and treasurer respectively, started out in printing and publishing with the major. In the early '30s the major . . . "

"Your father."

". . . my father . . . broke off to try the syndication business. He retained a small interest in the company, which was passed on to my stepmother, and we have 'first look' at any new properties they develop."

He frowned. "Properties they develop?"

"New comics characters. Anything they decide to publish in comic books, we have the opportunity to take out into newspaper syndication. It's only happened three times."

"But in a big way, right?"

"Well . . . yes. *Wonder Guy* and *Batwing*. And *Amazonia* is doing okay. Why?"

He shrugged. "Just gathering some background. That's the other reason I wouldn't've minded coming over and talking to your . . . do you prefer I refer to Miss Starr as your boss, or your stepmother?"

"I don't care. Commanding officer is fine, too . . . . Why are you gathering background on a suspicious death, if that's all it is?"

He cleared his throat. Sat forward. Found an open space on the desktop to fold his hands.

Serious time.

"Donny Harrison's death is a murder, Mr. Starr."

"Why don't you call me 'Jack.'"

"All right, Jack. You can call me Pat, if you like."

"I kind of prefer 'Captain.' It reminds me that even if I won the Silver Star in Oklahoma and all you could manage out of the Pacific was a Purple Heart and Ruptured Duck, well, nonetheless you still outrank me."

He just looked at me, clearly offended. But then he broke out laughing. "You are a hell of a piece of work, Jack. Hell of a one."

I wasn't laughing, but I almost was, and a smile was taking place on my face no matter how hard I told my mouth to behave itself.

"Captain," I said finally, leaning back, "I have to say I am impressed with you, and with the Homicide Bureau."

"Really."

"Really. It takes a crack detective to determine that a guy who falls on a cake knife has been murdered. Was a midget hiding under that table with the cake on it? And crawled out behind Donny and shoved him onto that knife and then scurried back under? Best theory I can come up with."

He wasn't laughing when he said, "Mr. Harrison wasn't killed by that cake knife; or, if he was, he would have been dead soon, anyway."

"Then . . . must have been a heart attack. He was a big fat guy, in case you haven't made it around to the morgue."

With an air of infinite patience, he said, "I was over at Roosevelt Hospital this morning, and I did see the body. And, yes, he was on the rotund side. But his girth had nothing to do with his cause of death."

I held up a "stop" palm. "I still don't see why a guy falling on a knife is 'suspicious,' in the first place. I mean, call Ripley's Believe It or Not!, fine; zany as hell, yes. But suspicious?"

"The suspicions came *after* the autopsy, which his wife requested."

Of course I knew Selma Harrison intended to take that step;

but Chandler had given me the impression the police department suggested or even required the procedure.

He was saying, "Except for a medical condition that Mr. Harrison kept in check, he was supposedly in good health."

"According to his wife . . . . What medical condition?"

He shook his head. "I'll get to that. A routine step in the autopsy procedure caused the hospital to notify the medical examiner's office."

"What routine step?"

"In the autopsy? A toxicity screen of the blood. Mr. Harrison had something unusual in his bloodstream—a quantity of a chemical compound, an organophosphate, highly poisonous, found chiefly in pesticides."

I sat forward. "Then Donny Harrison was poisoned?"

"That's the opinion of the pathologist."

"And he . . . he was either dead, or dying, or passing out, when he fell on that knife . . . ."

Chandler was nodding all through that. "Exactly. His symptoms were consistent with organophosphate poisoning—sweating, salivation, nausea, dizziness . . ."

My mind was whirling like the overhead fan blades. "If somebody put foul crap like that in his food, or drink, wouldn't Donny have tasted it?"

He shook his head. "The contents of his stomach did not include the pesticide. Ingestion was not the means of delivery."

"Well, how the hell *was* it delivered?"

"I'll duck that for the moment, Jack . . . but I will answer the question you posed earlier—what was the medical condition that

Mr. Harrison was 'keeping in check'? . . . I take it you weren't aware that Mr. Harrison was a diabetic."

I sat back. Shook my head. "I had no idea. Look, I wasn't close to the guy, particularly not in recent years. Did others, closer to him, know?"

"Definitely. Donny gave himself up to four shots of insulin a day, Jack—and he kept supplies of insulin, refrigerated of course, at three locations. Can you guess what those locations were?"

"Sure. His home, his office, and his mistress's. By refrigerated, do you mean . . . in the refrigerator?"

Chandler nodded. "A refrigerator at home, another in the break room at Americana headquarters and another in the kitchen at Miss Daily's Waldorf suite."

"And your theory is, a dosage of the insulin was fatally doctored?"

"Yes, or switched." He stopped rocking and made an elaborate openhanded gesture. "We think the last dose he took was . . . the last dose he took."

I thought about that for a few seconds. Then I asked, "Does the medical examiner say how long that pesticide mickey would take, before kicking in? In other words, did it have to be a dose he took at Miss Daily's, minutes before he stabbed himself?"

Chandler shook his head. "It might have taken up to several hours to take full effect, I'm told. That puts all three locations of the insulin in play."

Now I was shaking my head. "Christ, dozens of people had access. Scores. His wife and children and household staff, at home; his partners and employees at work; and all those guests at the birthday party at the Waldorf. Plus, at the latter, the Waldorf staffers he had in, to handle the party."

"Actually," Chandler said, "Miss Daily's suite might have been the hardest location for somebody to make a switch or doctor a bottle. The kitchen was the staging area for the Waldorf catering crew. So we have plenty of potential witnesses at that site."

I drew a deep breath and rolled my eyes. "Well, I wish you good luck and lots of patience. How many interviews does that bode?"

Chandler shrugged. "Eight Waldorf employees. Not so bad. But we have sixty-two at the party, and twenty-seven at Americana, and five at Harrison's home."

"Lucky you. You say, Harrison's diabetes was well known by friends and associates?"

His brow tightened. "I wouldn't say 'well known'—you were in his life, to some extent anyway, Jack, and you weren't aware . . . . Speaking of which, see if your stepmother knew about the condition, would you?"

"Glad to. But the people in Donny's daily life were all cognizant of his medical problem?"

"Yes."

"Hell, a Waldorf staffer wouldn't be."

"No, Jack, but someone who *was* could have hired one of them to do it."

"A catered poisoning?"

"Stranger things have happened."

I smirked. "Yeah, this is New York. Stranger things have probably happened since we sat down here. But where do I come in?"

He jabbed a forefinger my way. "You were the first to get to the body. You turned him over. Can you think of anything significant you might have noticed?"

"Yeah," I said, shifting in my chair, "I noticed the sweaty slob had a big significant knife in his heart. I'm a trained investigator myself, Captain. I wasn't about to miss that."

He grunted a small laugh. "Okay, smart-ass comedy aside . . . was there anything unusual?"

How was I supposed to avoid smart-ass comedy when this captain of homicide was asking me if there was anything unusual about a fat guy in a Wonder Guy costume with a cake knife in his chest?

"Well, there were no famous last words." I turned my hands palms up. "The guy was dead. Knife or poison, he was blue in the face and smiling up at God. Let's just hope nobody upstairs ever had a look at the Americana ledgers."

An eyebrow rose. "Speaking of which . . . among the guests were Harold Spiegel and Morris Shulman."

The hairs at the back of my neck did a tingly little dance. "They're the creators of Americana's top property. Why shouldn't they be there?"

He let out a short expulsion of air that was a sort of laugh. "Jack, I've been on this case exactly one morning . . . it's only been a *case* exactly one morning . . . and yet I already know that there's incredible animosity between Spiegel and Shulman and their late, I would guess, unlamented publisher."

I gave him a one-shoulder shrug. "Donny made a lot of friends. He was a guy who thought it was appropriate to throw himself a birthday party at his mistress's place and then invite the wife. Real prince of a guy. Prince as in the name of a dog, as in real son of a bitch."

"So you're saying Mrs. Harrison did it?"

"I'm not saying anything! I'm saying of the going-on one hundred names on the list of people you need to interview, probably half of them had a reason, if not a full-fledged motive, to push Donny off a high building and see if his Wonder Guy outfit could help him fly."

He inhaled. He exhaled. "I've already been told by four reliable sources that Harry Spiegel is an excitable, resentful little man."

"If you'd created *Wonder Guy*, and got half of one hundred thirty dollars for your trouble, wouldn't you be?"

"So you consider him, and his partner Shulman, credible suspects?"

"Harry Spiegel is an irritating, sweet little Jewish fourteen-year-old from Des Moines, Iowa, who never grew up. He is about as dangerous as a gumdrop. His partner is a quiet, unassuming, half-blind character who would give a mouse the cheese and toss the trap in the garbage. Get a grip, Captain."

His eyes were locked on mine. "You said it yourself—you were a cop, Jack. Trained investigator. Who do *you* like for the murder?"

I shoved back in the chair and it screamed a little on the wooden floor. Got to my feet, stuck my hat on my head and said, "Nice meeting you, Captain. We simply must get together again soon to swap old war stories."

He rose. "If I need to contact you . . ."

I got my billfold out of my hip pocket and found him a business card. "The top number is my office, the second one is my apartment. . . . If you want to buy nude photos of my stepmother, give me a ring."

He gave me one more smile, but you know what? This one looked forced.

Around quarter to four, I was back at the Starr Building, where Bryce informed me that Maggie was in the gym and that I was to join her there.

"Should I change into my gym shorts?"

Bryce's white teeth blossomed in the midst of the dark beard. "That's optional."

I laughed and said, "Shut up," and went through Maggie's office on into the gym, which was an even larger room, though a wall of mirrors along the left wall, cut by a ballet bar, exaggerated that.

Much of the floor was covered by tumbling mats, and an impressive array of the latest exercise equipment lined the wall opposite the mirror—a rowing machine, a stationary bicycle, a pulley with weights and (her latest addition) a treadmill—apparently riding on a bike to nowhere wasn't enough: she had to be able to walk nowhere, just as fast.

Some of these gizmos weren't even in the big-time commercial gyms yet: Maggie had charmed herself onto the testing lists of several top manufacturers. That treadmill had been developed in medical research, for instance.

Beyond the gym was a small sauna and two small dressing rooms with separate showers, one for her and one for me, since she generously made the gym available to her lowly stepson. Proof of this was over in the far right corner, a hanging punching bag that I pretended kept me in shape but in reality just helped vent my frustrations.

When I entered, Maggie—in black leotards that revealed a curvaceous figure most women would have killed for, rather than turned reclusive over—was on a slant board doing sit-ups.

I sat on the nearby bike, not pedaling, and waited for her to take a break. I don't know how many sit-ups she did before I got there, but I counted twenty-seven before she rolled off, grabbed a towel, patted down her face and said to me, "Well?"

I gave her a full rundown on what Captain Chandler had asked, and what I had answered—not word for word, but my memory is one of the most reliable things about me. She jumped rope through most of it and I was exhausted by the time she and I had finished.

"Take a break, why don't you?" I said. "You're killing me."

"Sissy," she said, and went over to a thermos and poured herself some ice water. "Want a sip?"

"No. Let's sit down, though."

A bench on the back wall, between the doors to the men's and women's dressing rooms, was our only option other than the floor. She sat with her hands on her knees and breathed deeply, but honestly she didn't seem winded or anything.

"So how's the weight?"

"One thirty-two," she said. "Miles to go before I sleep."

"Well, just the same, you need to come out of hibernation. Donny's funeral is tomorrow, you know. You should be there."

She shook her head and the red curls flicked sweat on me. "*You* can represent the company."

"Like hell." I took the towel from her and wiped her sweat off me.

"That's what vice presidents do, Jack: attend funerals."

"Swell. What else do vice presidents do?"

Her head swiveled and the green eyes fixed on me, unblinkingly; that pale, lightly freckled face of hers was intimidating in its beauty, and she hadn't a speck of makeup on. She looked young. About twelve.

But she sounded eternal as she asked, "What do *you* think a vice president in your situation should do?"

I took a deep breath. I looked anywhere but at her. I let the breath out.

"I'm afraid," I said, "a vice president in my situation ought to look into this goddamned murder."

"Why?" Nothing accusatory or argumentative—just *why*.

I shook my head wearily. "Chandler is looking hard at Harry Spiegel and Moe Shulman. If the boys did this, we ought to know about it as soon as possible, before we sign a new contract with them on that new strip. And if they didn't do this, we ought to help 'em out of this jam."

"That's noble."

"You know me, Maggie. Nobility is my middle name."

"Your middle name is Thomas. And I suspect 'Doubting' is squeezed in after the John . . . *But*—I agree with you."

Now I looked at her, only she was studying the matted floor. "Really," I said. "What in the hell's got into you, agreeing with me?"

"It's not nobility. The Starr Syndicate is in a spot. Two of our top talents are key murder suspects—if they did it, we have a publicity nightmare, at least a temporary one."

I snorted a laugh. "Not that temporary. Months. Well into next year. A trial and, God help us, executions. 'Wonder Guys Go to the Chair.' How many papers do you think the strip will be in after that?"

She sighed. "I could use a smoke."

"I thought you quit."

"I did. I don't want one. I could just use one."

"Oh."

"Don't you ever want a drink?"

"No more often than you want a smoke. Maggie, did you know Donny was diabetic?"

"Sure."

". . . I hate it when I'm the last to know."

The green eyes locked onto me again. "Jack, if the boys didn't do it, but are arrested, and sit in stir for weeks and maybe months, they'll look guilty enough for papers all over America to drop the *Wonder Guy* strip like a bad habit."

"Like smoking?"

"Not to mention, the longer this drags on, with all its connections to us—Americana and their employees and Rod Krane and that goofy guy writing *Amazonia*, and maybe the mob connections getting dredged up—we'll be the focus of ridicule and criticism and, well, nothing good."

"I agree," I said.

She frowned so hard a small crease revealed itself between her eyes. "What do you think of Chandler?"

"He seems fairly sharp. There's a lot that the Homicide Bureau and the New York City police department can accomplish that I can't—including interview all damn-near one hundred pertinent people . . . suspects and witnesses and what have you. And it's not like I have pathologists at my fingertips."

She put a hand on my shoulder; she rarely touched me, so I knew this was a big deal. "Maybe so, Jack, but you know the key players . . . and you know most of them personally, and can ask questions and get at things and places that the police can't."

"I agree with that, too. I think I see where you're going."

She stood, let out a deep breath, and walked to the rowing machine and climbed in. I followed along.

As she rowed, she said, "If . . . you . . . can . . . solve . . . this . . . thing . . . *fast* . . ."

"That would minimize the publicity damage," I said. "Even if Harry and/or Moe did do this thing . . . but, come on, Maggie— you can't really believe there's a chance either one of those tortured but gentle souls is capable of murder."

"There . . . must . . . be . . . one . . . other . . . thing . . . *I* . . . know . . . that . . . *you* . . . don't . . ."

"Such as?"

She stopped rowing and reached for her towel. She actually had worked up a sweat and gulped for wind a short while before answering.

"Such as Moe Shulman is a diabetic, too," she said. "Why the hell do you think he's going blind?"

Late that same afternoon, I passed through the mosaic-tiled foyer of the Waldorf and up the stairs into the lobby and past its imposing marble columns and formidable bronze lamps. On my way, mingling with the well-dressed mob as though I belonged, I glimpsed in at the elegant blue-and-white Wedgewood Room, from which emanated string-quartet supper music ("Laura," at the moment) that provided an inoffensively melodic counterpoint to the percussive hum of the bustling hotel.

What really caught my attention, however, were a couple of overstuffed goons in overstuffed chairs between potted plants with more personality and intelligence than either chair occupant. A pockmarked, putty-faced guy in a green fedora, brown tie with blue amoeba blobs, and double-breasted brown suit—whose jacket was even more oversize than its owner, to disguise the rod under his arm—was reading *Variety*; maybe that rumored Damon

Runyon musical was casting. This specimen I'd never seen before, but the ferret-faced character beside him, in a white fedora and floral tie and cream-color summer suit whose underarm jacket bulge was undisguised, I knew just enough to wish I didn't.

Legs crossed to show off the black socks that clashed with his white shoes, Big Jim—an oddity whose skinny face belied his full-back's form—was reading *The Racing News*. I knew him a little—he was Frank Calabria's number one bagman.

As I walked by, Big Jim's beady eyes rose above the edge of the newspaper and met my unbeady ones. I nodded. He nodded.

Buddies.

The presence of Big Jim and his putty-faced pal, near and in sight of the bank of elevators, meant their boss was up a tower in his sweetie's suite. Calabria's setup with his longtime ex-showgirl mistress had supposedly inspired Donny Harrison's similar one with Honey Daily.

Coincidentally, Honey Daily accounted for my presence at the Waldorf—I sure wasn't here for the apples-and-walnut salad, being an iceberg lettuce kind of guy.

Not that Miss Daily had summoned me: this was my idea, and I hadn't warned her with a phone call. My limited experience on murder cases, during my MP days, told me such an investigation was not aided by making appointments with suspects. Dropping by unannounced may be rude, and it may risk finding nobody home; but the benefits for a detective are considerable, starting with gaining a psychological edge on an individual who hasn't had time to prepare for your interview.

That said, I didn't exactly consider Honey Daily a suspect. I didn't exactly not consider her a suspect, either, but then I also wasn't planning to interview her . . . exactly.

I felt we'd hit it off interestingly and well at Donny's birthday party, up to where he dropped dead onto that knife, anyway. And I hoped we could pick up where we left off, now that she was un-attached and might need a sympathetic shoulder, said shoulder being attached to the rest of me, should she need any other sym-pathetic body part.

Soon I'd gone up the elevator and down the hall and up to the door of her suite, and knocked. The door had a small peephole above its gold numerals, and I must have been approved for entry, because as I raised my knuckles to try again, the door swung in-ward halfway and she filled the available space with herself, decked out in a black dressing gown, her fetchingly mussed-up blonde hair brushing shoulders whose pinkness could not be dis-guised by filmy black.

"I remember you," she said, martini in hand, smirky smile on full lips.

Was she just a little drunk? I couldn't be sure. It wasn't as though she'd answered my knock in a negligee—the dressing gown was layers of sheer stuff that didn't obscure her shape but also didn't put it on display. Still, these were not the usual widow's weeds; of course, she wasn't a widow—kept woman's weeds?

"I was in the neighborhood," I said. I nodded down the hall. "Returning a lost puppy to a little old lady who lives down next to the ice machine."

"I like you," she said. "You're silly."

Where had I heard that before? As she bid me enter with a slightly unsteady sweeping gesture, making room for me, I remembered: Tweety Bird to Sylvester the Cat in a cartoon that did not turn out well for the cat.

She shut the door behind us and I was moving into the entry way, footsteps echoing on green marble. I wheeled to look at her; she was slumped against the white door in her black dressing gown, red-nailed hand leaning on the gold doorknob, other hand regally if precipitously holding the martini, making a somber pinup. On either side of her was a white slab of something with a Grecian bust on top. The walls were coral with white wood trim, and at my left was a bronze-framed mirror and a white table with fresh flowers on it, also white. At right was another white door, presumably to a closet.

Her baby blues, bearing a red filigree, found their way to my face. "Are you here to take advantage of me? Or to try and cheer me up?"

I shrugged. "Maybe it'll cheer you up if I took advantage of you."

She laughed, a little more than that rated, and it echoed in the space, giving the laughter bottom but not disguising the ragged edge of hysteria up top.

I went over to her and took an elbow and walked her into the living room, almost dragging her over the fluffy white carpet.

The big high-ceilinged area looked strikingly different than it had during Donny's party, and not just because sixty-some people were no longer wandering around in it. Hotel elves had come in after the cops left to put the world of the suite right again, some furniture having been added back in, and all of it rearranged. The white baby grand was gone, rolled out with the Negro pianist.

Down toward the end of the living room, through open French doors at left, extended a large dining room, and where its long table had been covered with a linen cloth and arrayed with hors d'oeuvres at the party was now bare, sleek dark wood adorned only with a centerpiece of white and pink flowers.

Meanwhile, back in the living room, the two emerald leather chairs that had been here and there at the periphery, and a couch that had lined a wall, were back in what I presumed was their usual arrangement: the pair of chairs side by side and facing the couch across a glass coffee table, next to the marble fireplace and its mirror over the mantel.

I escorted her to that couch, near where a martini glass rested on the glass table, making a wet circle. The air-conditioning was on high, almost uncomfortably so, and my mind automatically and ridiculously looked at the fireplace and wished it were going.

I sat next to her and she nestled against me, grabbing on to my arm like a *Titanic* survivor clinging to a floating chunk of deck chair. The lighting was subdued, with only one of several lamps on, its square shade upheld by a female Balinese dancer on a white table; a male Balinese dancer was doing the same thing with an identical shade on an identical table, but in darkness, past a white door down the wall.

The other day I hadn't noticed that the modernity of the furnishings and the general decor—the drawn drapes on a big window we faced were light green with a coral geometric pattern—had these faux touches of antiquity. The lamp tables and a couple of spare chairs had an Egyptian feel, and a couple more disembodied white-plaster Greek noggins on pedestals stared at us from this corner or that one.

At the same time, even as my nostrils tingled with her Chanel No. 5, I saw the ghosts of the guests of the birthday party, wandering around and even through the furniture—Donny in his cape and sweat-soaked superhero long johns flying from attendee to attendee, Rod Krane in his gray Brooks Brothers rewarding the room with his presence, Harry Spiegel and Moe Shulman in their wrinkled off-the-rack numbers, Selma Harrison off to one side with her floral tent a stark contrast to Louis Cohn's maitre d's tuxedo.

Right over by those drapes—they'd been open onto the city at the party, the Empire State in the background—the table had stretched with Donny's birthday cake. With the lighting so dim, a discolored patch on the floor was hard to make out, and at first I thought it was my imagination.

I was sitting up.

She said, not quite slurring, "Liquor cart's in the bedroom. You want something? . . . Oh, but you don't drink."

"You have any Coca-Cola?"

"Sure. It's in the kitchen." She pointed and her red-nailed forefinger tickled the air. "Over there."

She indicated the white door between the two white tables with the Balinese dancer lamps.

"I'll get it myself," I said, and rose.

I glanced at her, and she was slumped back into an emerald leather cushion, eyes closed, a provocative pile of blonde hair, pink flesh and black taffeta.

But I took a small detour, to see if my imagination was working overtime or if there really was a big fat stain on the plush white carpeting, right where Donny had fallen. I crouched like Sherlock Holmes trying to find a magnifying glass he'd dropped, finding instead that (despite the lack of light) my eyes were doing fine.

An area roughly the size of dead Donny had discolored the carpet, all right, turning it a sort of sick gray, as best I could tell in this lighting. That knife had gone in Donny and held the blood in, the cork in a bottle—there'd been precious little spillage, and the knife had not been removed when the body had been, by the ambulance boys—I remembered that clearly, since it was one more bizarre aspect of that offbeat birthday party.

Then why was the carpet so discolored? And, anyway, blood wouldn't have made this gray smear. Had the cops noticed this last night? Had Chandler been here today? I rose and glanced over at the couch where Honey appeared asleep.

Shrugging to myself, I went through the white door into a white kitchen—medium-size, but it had probably been crowded when the Waldorf caterers were using it as a staging station. Much of the floor space was taken up by a red-topped Formica table with four red plastic-upholstered chairs, and two walls were cabinets above counter with doors below, another wall was given over to a little more counter and cabinets but mostly double sink and a big refrigerator. And a second door connected to the dining room.

Still, the space was small enough that you'd imagine any guest who ducked in to fiddle with something in the refrigerator would get noticed.

Speaking of the fridge, I checked it to see if any insulin bottle was still in there. It wasn't—Chandler must have been here today, or his men; the cops last night wouldn't likely have thought to take the bottle for testing, Donny's demise still seeming an accident.

The refrigerator didn't have much of anything in it but a half-gone bottle of milk, some veggies, half a carton of eggs, some cold cuts and bottles of 7-Up and Coke. I took one of the latter, found an opener in a drawer and a glass in a cabinet and poured and thought.

I set the fizzing glass of Coke on the counter, found a small sharp knife in another drawer, and fished around for longer than I'd have liked in other drawers until I came across recipe cards, each in a little yellow envelope fronted by the beaming, beautiful and utterly sexless mug of that fictional housewife, Betty Crocker.

One of these envelopes I liberated, slipping it in my suitcoat pocket, dropping the knife in the other, finally exiting the kitchen into the dimly lighted living room, leaving the glass of Coke behind.

The slumping Honey looked asleep. Certainly her eyes were closed and she was breathing regular and heavy.

So, I crept back to that suspicious stain and knelt again and cut off a few tufts of discolored carpet, tucking them away inside the Betty Crocker envelope, which went back into one suitcoat pocket, even as the little sharp knife went into the other suitcoat pocket.

Rising from my knee like a rejected suitor, I noted Honey's continuing sleep state, and went back into the kitchen, returning the knife to its drawer and reemerging with my Coke.

I resumed my position at her side on the couch and her arms found my nearest one and clung again.

"Hey," I said.

Her eyelids fluttered.

"Hey you," I said.

The eyelids fluttered some more and opened enough to peer up at me. "I know you," she said. "You're that flirt."

"That's right. When's the last time you ate?"

"I don't remember."

"Today?"

"I . . . I don't think so."

"How many martinis have you had?"

"I . . . I didn't even get out of bed till four."

"Four P.M.?"

She nodded and the blonde hair bounced, looking nicely mussed. That was when I realized she didn't have a smidge of makeup on and still looked as glamorous as an *Esquire* layout.

"You slept all day?" I asked.

"I . . . I had help."

"What kind of help?"

"Kind in a bottle."

"Booze?"

She shook her head. "Pills."

I took her by both shoulders and made her look at me. "You didn't overdose, did you, you little fool?"

"I didn't overdose. I'm no fool. Do I still like you?"

"You tell me."

"I only had three martinis. That's not so much."

"Without having eaten? After God knows how many seda-
tives? You couldn't be drunker."

"Sure I could. Your name is Jack, isn't it?"

I got up and turned on a few more lamps. Not enough to turn
the living room into a blazing high noon, but plenty to make her
squint in annoyance and yell, "Hey!"

"We're getting you something to eat."

She gestured vaguely, presumably toward a phone, though I
hadn't spotted any in the room. "Call down."

"Not room service, a real meal." I went over and lifted her
bodily off the sofa. "Go put some clothes on. Where's the bedroom?"

She pointed to another white door, over past the drapes, to the
right.

I walked her over there, past the stain and the drapes and more
white Egyptian chairs and into a big darkened bedroom, the color
scheme blue and white. The only light came from a bathroom
whose door stood open, sending a shaft of white across the unmade blue satin bedspread—a double bed, with a matching satin
tufted headboard.

"Get dressed," I said.

She was over against the wall at right by double closet doors
next to a dressing table with round mirror and round stuffed stool.
Arrayed on a glass-topped table were half the fancy cut-glass bottles of perfume and such like in Manhattan. Feet planted but
weaving, she studied me.

"I don't feel like . . . like getting dressed up."

I was sitting on the bed, using the white phone on her white nightstand. "I didn't say get dressed up. You need a reservation a week ahead for the Starlight Roof, even if I could afford it."

She squinted at me. "Where then? I don't feel like leaving the hotel."

"Shut up," I said. I had the Oasis Lounge on the line. "Table for two in half an hour? . . . Fine . . . Starr." I hung up. "We're going down to Tony Sarg's Oasis. Dress accordingly. A pith helmet maybe."

That made her laugh. She *was* drunk.

I got up. "I'll go drink my Coke. If you fall on your keister, try to make a lot of noise, would you? So I can ride to your rescue?"

She stuck out her tongue at me. "I dare you to stay and watch."

"I can do that, but I'll have to call down and get a later reservation."

With an elaborate, taunting shrug, she brought her hands to the bowed black sash at her waist and began undoing the dressing gown.

Rolling my eyes for nobody's benefit but yours, I went out and sat on the sofa by the unlit fireplace and drank my Coke. Suddenly it didn't seem all that air-conditioned in the place.

Twenty minutes later, she emerged from her bedroom. Maybe she hadn't wanted to "dress up," but I had no doubt she would have been welcome at the Starlight Roof. Her dress, which stopped just below her knees, was black but her shoulders and midriff were bare under misty black lace, her arms mostly bare, too. A simple strand of pearls was at her pink throat, and now her lips were rouged, red as blood.

I was already on my feet. "You look swell."

"Thanks. I feel . . . better."

"So do I," I said, going over to her. "Listen, a meal will do you good. Way you're going, you'll either starve yourself, or drown in martinis."

She managed a smile. The blue eyes didn't look so bloodshot now, either—she must have used drops. "I didn't fall on my keister, Mr. Starr . . . Jack. But you did ride to my rescue. Thank you."

"I'm available twenty-fours," I said, "to beautiful women, anyway."

The Tony Sarg Oasis, off the lobby, was more cocktail lounge than restaurant, the curving wall decorated by a whimsical mural (courtesy of the cartoonist whose name graced the place) of Disneyesque animals—gin-guzzling giraffes, reeling rodents, tipsy tigers. A small bandstand of violinists and cellists put out the room's signature Hungarian pop rhapsodies, with the main menu item (beyond sandwiches) reflecting the music with a tasty goulash that was a favorite of mine.

So, as we sat beneath a fan-dancing elephant, I ordered this hearty specialty for both of us, plus another Coke for me and coffee for the lady. She did not object but requested cream. Thus it was that I set about to sober up this female in the midst of fullscale cocktail lapping.

"I notice you don't smoke," I said.

"No," she said. "Smoking ages a woman. I notice you don't, either."

"I used to. But for me, smoking and drinking went together, so when drinking went, so did the Lucky Strikes."

She gestured to all the booze consumption as well as the haze of cigarette smoke. "Doesn't it bother you, being in this atmosphere?"

"No. After you've been off the sauce a while, you start to enjoy the edge you get, being one of the sober few in a soused-up joint like this."

She gave me that smiling-mouth-frowning-eyes expression that she should have patented. "Was that some kind of veiled dig?"

"No. You seem sober enough right now. Just getting up and moving around and getting dressed was enough to set you on the straight and narrow. When you get some chow down you, you'll be a new woman."

"Didn't you like the old one?"

"Nothing old about you, Honey. You're still fine with me calling you 'Honey,' aren't you?"

"Jack, I'd be offended if you didn't."

The Coke and coffee came.

I sipped at the icy glass, then said, "I am sorry for your loss. I know Donny meant a lot to you."

She lifted her coffee cup to her lips and studied me over its rim while she drank; she was looking for sarcasm in my words and my face, and couldn't find any.

"Thank you," she said, setting the cup down steadily. "I know Donny wasn't your favorite person."

"He was a lot of people's *not* favorite person." I sat forward, spoke as softly as I dared, competing with "Golden Earrings" in the background. "Honey, am I the first person to drop around today?"

Now just her eyes frowned. "Didn't I tell you? That's how, I mean, *who* woke me up, around four—a Captain Chandler, and some other police detective."

"I see. Then you're aware that Donny's death . . ."

"Was a murder? Yes. Why do you think I was hitting the martinis so hard?" She shook her head, the blondeness bouncing. "You pop enough pills to sleep just short of forever, to try get away from the . . . the *awfulness* of losing somebody you care about. Then some goddamn policeman comes around and makes it . . . makes it even worse."

Her voice was trembling but her eyes were steady; no tears. Maybe she'd cried every tear she had out of her. Or maybe she was just steeling herself, digging into the capacity she had for living thirty-some years and not wrinkling that lovely mug an iota.

"Was Chandler . . ." I tried to find the word. ". . . unpleasant? Rough on you?"

"No, no. He was nice enough. Very gentlemanly. You know, he's even cuter than you are."

"That's a matter of opinion," I said. "And, anyway, you don't have to rub it in."

She smiled; her teeth might have been too large for some people's tastes, but not mine—big and white and beautiful, framed in full red lips. "Didn't mean to hurt your feelings, Jack."

"I'm dainty. Delicate. Remember that."

"I'll try to." She was still smiling, though she'd put the teeth away. "All Captain Chandler did was inform me about the murder, and ask a few questions, and asked if I minded if he looked around. I said of course not."

No wonder he was so goddamned nice—Honey was undoubtedly one of his top suspects, and the cute cop had been allowed to search her apartment without a warrant.

I asked, "Did he take anything with him?"

"Yes. Several bottles of insulin that were in my refrigerator. Donny had diabetes, you know. Donny always kept several bottles on hand at the apartment."

"And at work? And at home?"

She nodded. "He always said, 'Boy Scouts like me are always prepared.' He had such a wonderful sense of humor."

Well, that was depressing to hear. Honey Daily, who laughed at all my jokes, found Donny Harrison a riot. I was going to have to rethink my material.

The goulash came, and was as usual delicious. Honey damn near wolfed hers down, so this had been a good call. I even talked her into a little dessert, some cheesecake and strawberries, not Lindy's worthy, but not bad.

Our talk remained small over the meal and cheesecake. I learned that she had grown up in Cleveland, came to New York to try to be an actress. She admitted her good looks got her plenty of auditions, but that her lack of talent meant the only offers were the kind she could have gotten anywhere, from a Cleveland soda fountain to any New York street corner.

She had switched showbiz gears and taken dancing lessons for a while—her parents, who ran a haberdashery back home, had agreed to stake her for a year out here to pursue her dream; but her terpsichorean talents weren't any better than her thespian ones. Finally she and another failed actress signed up for a secretarial school, and here Honey excelled. After graduation, she worked for several bosses, but meeting Donny in 1940 had changed her life.

A waiter had taken the empty cheesecake plates away, and brought Honey more coffee and me some iced tea—Coke and cheesecake don't mix—and I began to probe a little deeper. We were better acquainted now, and she was as sober as a judge, ruling out the high percentage of drunken New York judges, that is.

I squeezed the lemon into my tea and asked, "What does Donny's death do to your . . . situation?"

"Nothing, really."

"Nothing? You mean, ycu'll continue living in a Waldorf suite . . . . I don't mean to overstep, but how is that possible?"

She frowned enough now to show the potential for wrinkling. "You *are* overstepping a little, Jack."

I shifted in my seat, leaned forward to be heard over the syrupy "Gypsy Love Song," the little string combo taking Victor Herbert way too seriously. "Honey, I want to be on the up and up with you. I'm looking into Donny's murder."

Her eyes, tight with confusion and wide with sudden distrust, bore into me. "You're . . . what? *Why?* . . . That sounds wrong, *of course* I want Donny's murder looked into, and whoever did this awful thing brought to justice, but . . . that's the *police's* job. Isn't it?"

"Yes, it is. But I'm licensed investigator, Honey. And among my duties for the Starr Syndicate is protecting its interests."

She tilted her head and narrowed her eyes. "What interests?"

"The Americana comic properties we syndicate. And their creators—like Spiegel and Shulman, for instance."

"Why them?"

"Come on, Honey. You must know they're bound to be prime suspects in this thing. Donny made his share of enemies, but they're at the top of the list."

She untilted her skull but kept the eyes narrow. "And you want to . . . what? *Help* them, or . . . what?"

"If they're innocent, I want them cleared, fast. If they're guilty, I want them caught the same way. Minimize the damage to the interested party."

"Interested party," she said, and sipped coffee, "being the Starr Syndicate."

"Frankly, yes. I have no doubt that Captain Chandler is competent, and . . ." I nodded to the fan-dancing elephant. ". . . cute as these cartoon critters. But I know the comics business, and the people involved, better than he ever will."

One eyebrow hiked. "And . . . the people involved who you *don't* know all that well? Like me, for instance? Them you need to cultivate?"

I raised both palms, chest high, in surrender. "I'm being on the up and up, Honey, like I said. Nobody on earth knew Donny better than you—in fact, I'm convinced you knew things about him, knew sides of him, no one else did."

She swallowed—not her coffee, just swallowed. "I was very fond of him."

"And he was fond of you." I leaned forward again. "But fond

enough to remember you in his will? Despite how that might look?"

Her eyes and nostrils flared. I braced for getting coffee splashed in my face, but she drew in several breaths and finally said, "I'm a suspect?"

"Of course you are. Hell, so am I. I was there, wasn't I, when the murder happened?"

"*Happened*, Jack? Donny's murder didn't, didn't 'happen'— somebody *did* it. And it wasn't me. I . . . I loved Donny, in a way. I wasn't *in* love with him, but he was sweet to me and good to me and I saw, yes, I saw sides of him nobody else ever did."

Now I sipped coffee, trying to calm the conversation. I needed to set a pace quick enough to get answers that weren't overly thought out, and slow enough not to rush her into irritation.

I said, "What I'd really like to do is rule you out, and then make an ally of you."

She actually laughed a little; a bitter edge to it, but a laugh. "You're Nick, I'm Nora? No thanks."

"I'm not looking for a partner. I just need you to answer some questions."

"Haven't I been?"

"Yes. And I appreciate that. But you didn't answer my question about Donny's will."

She shrugged. The strings were having a go at "Wandering Gypsy Girl." She said, "I'm not in his will."

I squinted at her through the cigarette smoke. "But you said your life wouldn't be interrupted . . . ."

She raised her chin, very dignified. Or trying to be. "Years ago Donny set up a trust fund for me. It's entirely mine, and generates enough money for the rest of my life to keep me in . . . comfort."

"Did . . . excuse me, I have to ask . . . did Donny's death mean you can access the principal?"

She took no apparent offense. "No. When I reach age fifty . . . I'm thirty-three now . . . that automatically comes into effect. I believe Donny did assume he'd be gone by then, and that I should have control over my own life."

I drew a breath. Let it out. "Another personal question. Do you pay for the Waldorf suite yourself, out of the money the trust fund generates?"

Quickly she shook her head. "That's taken care of by Americana. I have a contract with Americana as Donny's executive secretary; it, too, is set up to run until I'm fifty. My 'salary' is the cost of the suite, set up for any increases at the hotel to be compensated by Americana."

"What if Louis Cohn just . . . fires you?"

"If I'm let go, according to that contract, Americana pays me a lump sum of $150,000. I don't think Louis is likely to exercise that . . . and if he does, well, I'll move on with all that money."

"I see. Donny really did look out for you."

"Yes." Her tone was mildly defensive. "And you can see that I don't really improve my situation by having him gone."

I sat back. My mind spun with possibilities. Finally I said, "I'm going to have to seem impolite again. I'm sorry."

"Go on."

"Suppose you were sick of Donny. Suppose you secretly

93

loathed him. Hated having to . . . deal with him and his, excuse me, needs—"

She'd started vigorously shaking her head halfway through that. "No, no, no, that's ridiculous. I was very fond of him. He was like a big, generous uncle to me."

The *come-sit-on-Uncle's-lap-sweetie* kind.

Again I leaned forward. "Did Chandler ask you about any of this?"

"About . . . Donny's will, and my . . . situation?"

"That's right."

"No. Not at all."

I sighed. "Well, he'll get around to it. The fact that you will continue to get Donny's money, and to live in that suite, without having to put up with him and his—"

"I didn't look at it that way!"

"Well, Chandler will. Honey, your best course of action is to trust me. To tell me anything you know about Donny that might have . . . no nice way to say it . . . made somebody have wanted to murder him."

She was breathing hard. "Could we go back upstairs? I don't want to talk about this here, anymore."

"Sure."

Within ten minutes we were again seated on her sofa by that cold fireplace. I had allowed her to fetch herself a martini, which she was not by any means gulping.

Her feet were up on the glass table—she had kicked off her black heels—and her nyloned legs were crossed. She was sipping the martini and staring into nothing particular.

Then she said, "There's . . . something you should know."

"Okay."

She swung those baby blues my way. If she were any lovelier, I'd have thrown myself out her window. "I . . . I know someone who might have wanted Donny dead."

I knew a dozen or more, but said, "Who?"

She looked away again. "I don't want you to think badly of me."

"My opinion of you isn't half as important as Captain Chandler's and the state of New York's."

". . . Donny only spent two nights a week with me. It was . . . very regular—Monday and Thursday. Mostly we were here. Sometimes we went out, to a show, to Twenty-one, somewhere. We went to the restaurants and attractions here in the hotel, of course. But it was a . . . limited relationship. And, unless he . . . and sometimes we . . . were traveling, it was Monday, Thursday, like clockwork."

"Why is that?"

"He had excuses arranged, work-related, for his wife and family. And he was a good husband and father, and spent lots of time with Selma and his son and daughter. He would even cancel a Monday or Thursday with me, if one of his kids had a school event or synagogue function or something."

What a guy, our Donny.

"Okay," I said. She was clearly having trouble spitting something out. "Where are you headed, Honey?"

She sipped the martini. Leaned forward to set it down. Leaned back and folded her arms over the black halter-top-like portion of her dress. "I had my own life. Which Donny didn't know about. But I . . . I had my own life."

Oh. A Tuesday, Wednesday, Friday, Saturday, Sunday life.

"Other men?"

She nodded curtly.

"Anybody . . . in particular?"

She heaved a sigh; a really, really big one. "Yes. I think you know him . . . Rod Krane."

I restrained myself from blurting, *That jerk?*

Instead I asked, "Are you . . . still seeing him?"

"No! He's a jerk."

Ah. One for my side . . . .

"I mean," she said, "he can be a charmer, and he's handsome and has a nice way about him, till . . . till you find out he's mostly in love with himself."

"You broke it off with Krane?"

"Yes . . . about . . . about two weeks ago."

"And Rod didn't like that?"

"No . . . not at all. He kept calling. Kept threatening to tell Donny about us, if I didn't take him back."

If Krane were the corpse, Honey would have a hell of a motive. Unfortunately, the *Batwing* creator was still breathing . . . .

She was saying, "And I know *Rod* despised Donny. Had utter contempt for Donny. He kept saying he was really going to . . . what did he say exactly? Stick it to him."

Or to his insulin bottle, maybe?

"Honey, can you think of anybody else who had a particular reason to want Donny gone?"

"Probably my list is about the same as yours, Jack. What about Louie Cohn?"

"What about him?" I shrugged. "I thought the two of them were joined at the hip. Donny and Louie, brothers in business."

She shook her head, firmly. "I don't have to tell you they were opposites, in personality and approach. Louie thinks Americana is going to grow and change, in this postwar world."

"How do you know this?"

"Donny told me. He said Louie was getting big for his britches, getting uppity, with unrealistic dreams about where Americana Comics was heading."

"I'm not sure I follow."

"Sure you do. Louie has always thought Donny was an embarrassment—loud, an old-fashioned back slapper, and really past his time, out of step, out of place in this great new sophisticated world of business."

She had a point. I could see it. Already I was glad I'd talked to her, first.

"Jack, would you turn those lamps off? They're hurting my eyes."

"Sure," I said.

I got up and did that.

When I returned, the only light in the room was coming from the open door to the bedroom.

As I settled in on the sofa, she moved closer to me, so close that I just had to slip my arm around her.

"You think I'm terrible, don't you?" she said. It was just a question, no little-girl voice, no self-pity.

"No. I think you're beautiful."

"I know I'm beautiful. I'm afraid you think I'm *terrible*, which is something altogether different."

"I think . . . I think you've learned to look after yourself in a tough town."

She snuggled closer. That Chanel No. 5 scent still clung to her, and my nostrils. "You could say that about a whore, Jack."

I almost said, *Some of my best friends are whores*, but luckily my mind vetoed the motion.

"I'm not in the judgment business," I said. "I'm in the comics game."

She touched my cheek; her hand was cold and my cheek grew hot. Then she kissed me on the mouth, a long kiss, soft and sweet and, right at the end there, her tongue flicked at mine.

"I'm not drunk," she said.

"I know you aren't."

"But I am lonely and upset."

I kissed her. Short but sweet . . . .

"If I asked you to keep me company tonight," she whispered, "would you?"

"Sure. I could . . . camp out on this couch."

"I mean . . . I don't want to be alone, tonight. I don't want to sleep alone. And I don't want to have to take any more pills . . . . We don't have to . . . *do* anything. Just keep me company, Jack. Keep me warm. Just, you know . . . cuddle."

"No promises," I said, and kissed her again.

Plus, she could cook.

Despite the meager contents of her refrigerator, Honey Daily whipped up a light delicious omelet that we shared, with a side of buttered toast and coffee for her and tea for me.

Apparently I'd cuddled her out of mourning, because she was in another gauzy dressing gown but this time white with pink here and there, some of it ribbons, some of it her. Her mood had brightened, as well.

Conversation ran to smiles and giggles, the sort of morning-after shared embarrassment of two people who didn't know each other all that well and just shared the most intimate of human acts. And I don't mean an omelet.

But when I helped her clear the table and transport the dishes and silverware to the sink, she turned to again show me how lovely that blonde-framed heart-shaped face could look sans makeup, and to ask, "Do you know Will Hander? I mean, does the Starr Syndicate deal with him at all?"

"Yes," I said to the first part of her question, "and no," to the second.

She spoke up a little as she ran water over each dirty dish. "I just ask because it's a fairly open secret that Will is the co-creator of *Batwing*."

"I've heard that rumor," I admitted.

"No rumor," she said. "More tea?"

"Sure."

"Shall we take it out into the living room?"

We did, and soon we were seated back on that couch, her cup of coffee and mine of tea on the glass table. The suite's atmosphere had changed entirely, the geometric drapes drawn to let in mote-sprinkled sunshine and to reveal a dazzling cityscape highlighted by the Empire State. Also highlighted was that gray corpse-size smear on the floor.

Honey said, "Understand I didn't get this from Rod—if you ask him, you'll get a very different story. But Donny always said that Will and Rod created *Batwing* together, only because of sleazy tactics on the part of Rod and his lawyer father, Will got taken."

"Donny knew this, and didn't do anything about it?"

"Right. He said it wasn't *his* fault that Will was stupid, and Rod was slick. But he said Will had been hounding him about it lately. Making ridiculous demands."

I nodded. "I don't remember seeing Will at the birthday party."

"Because he wasn't there! Don and Louie rarely invited any of the talent, but Rod Krane and Spiegel and Shulman had contracts coming up, and represented the top properties, so they were an exception."

"I see."

She shrugged. "Hander was an unlikely guest in any event, considering how he and Donny had been getting along lately, or I should say hadn't been getting along."

I knew Will Hander had been the primary writer on *Batwing*, both the comic book and the strip, since the very beginning. But it was common practice for artists like Rod to hire freelance writers, and also to hire assistant and ghost artists, and yet still take all the credit—you think Disney draws all those ducks and mice himself?

So having help on *Batwing* was hardly unusual. If anything, the shared Spiegel and Shulman credit on *Wonder Guy* was the oddity.

I was just starting to follow up with something when a knock, knock, knock at the door startled both of us.

Checking my watch—8:30—I said, "Little early for visitors, isn't it?"

But she was already up and moving past me, in a rustle of white taffeta, saying, "I'll see who it is."

I was only barely presentable, in my shirtsleeves with no tie and an unshaven mug. My hostess had been good enough to provide a brand-new toothbrush as well as access to her tube of Ipana, so my breath was no danger to the civilized world. And I'd been offered the use of Honey's shower, but instead had merely splashed some water on my face in the bathroom sink, and figured I'd just head back to my own apartment for the amenities.

But, still, I was in no fit state to receive company, and that wasn't even factoring in embarrassment for Honey for having this unshaven obvious houseguest . . . or suite guest or . . .

Out in the entryway, I heard her say, "Mr. Morella," couldn't make out the rest and then a big guy in a chauffeur's uniform came striding on in. A broad-shouldered forty-ish character, he had a strong chin and dark handsome features undercut by the small, almost black eyes hugging his roman nose, under careless black slashes of eyebrow.

He planted himself over by one of the Balinese-dancer lamps and took off his cap. The uniform was a light green and went with the general green-and-coral decor, which still didn't make him seem to belong here.

"Mr. Starr," he said, with a nod. He had a pleasant baritone but Sinatra had nothing to worry about.

I got to my feet. "Hank Morella—haven't seen you for ages. Don't stand on ceremony—it's still 'Jack.' "

"I'm here to pick up Mr. Harrison's things," he said.

Honey moved past him, and me, muttering, "Couldn't this have waited?"

At the bedroom door, she said to me, "Jack, I won't be long—I just have to gather Donny's things for his driver."

"No big deal," I said with a shrug.

I asked Morella if he wanted some coffee. He said no, just standing there frozen with his chauffeur's cap fig-leafed in front of him. He wore no gloves but did have the kind of black leather boots that had made the Nazis so darn stylish.

"For Christ's sake, Hank," I said, "come over and take a load off."

He thought about that for a moment, then lumbered over and sat opposite me on one of the emerald chairs, cap in his lap.

"How's Mrs. Harrison holding up?" I asked.

"Okay, considering." He was perched on the edge of the comfy chair. "How is Miss Daily doing?"

"Okay, considering. Were you here for the party, Hank?"

He shook his head, but then contradicted himself with, "Yes, but I waited downstairs. In the lobby." Again he shook his head, only in a different way. "That was one of the . . . awkward ones."

"Donny dying? Yeah, damned awkward."

"I . . . I didn't mean that." He sighed. "I don't know if you know it, but I do as much driving for Mrs. Harrison as for Mister. More, really."

Noise from the bedroom indicated Honey wasn't bringing a gentle touch to the gathering of Donny's things.

"I didn't know that," I said. "How did the Harrisons split you up?"

He shrugged. "I didn't drive Mr. Harrison in to work, hardly ever—he took the ferry and caught a cab, unless he knew he was going to have meetings, and then I drove him. Otherwise I stayed around home—Mrs. Harrison don't drive, you see."

"Ah. Then why do I have the impression that you're on the Americana payroll?"

He frowned. "Where'd you hear that?"

"Hank," I said patiently, "the major was in business with Donny and Louie. And the Starr Syndicate is in business with Americana."

"Oh. Sure." He shifted in the chair. "Mostly I work for the

family. I do everything from cut the grass to get the dry cleaning. I guess . . . it'll *all* be for the family, now."

"So where do you live then, Hank? Out on Long Island?"

"Yes, I live over their garage. That's better than it sounds—a real nice apartment. Triple garage."

"How many cars do the Harrisons have?"

"Just the one Caddy. But there's all kinds of junk out in that garage." He frowned. "What I meant was, I have a nice big space up over there."

"Swell. What was Donny like to work for?"

"He was all right." Morella shrugged. "He wasn't no saint, but somebody was out of line, killing him."

"Don't go out on a limb, Hank."

He didn't get that; the little dark eyes in the otherwise handsome mug were like two raisins on a slab of cinnamon bread. Or maybe I still had breakfast on the mind.

Looking a little flushed, Honey came in, a fetching if slightly absurd sight in her filmy dressing gown with a big brown leather suitcase in either hand, like she was taking a sudden trip.

She lugged them over and dropped them, heavily, next to Morella's chair. "Here. What's she going to do with them? Synagogue rummage sale?"

He swallowed, turning the cap in his hands like a steering wheel. "I don't know, Miss Daily. I was just supposed pick his stuff up."

"Well?" she asked, hands on hips, eyes and nostrils flaring. "You waiting for a tip?"

He swallowed. "No, ma'am." He rose, nodded to me, said, "Nice seeing you, Jack," and she stepped back to give him room as he got hold of the suitcases and trundled off. Shaking her head, she tromped after him disgustedly, and I guess got the door for him. I couldn't see the foyer from where I sat.

The door slammed, and she came over and sat next to me and her arms were folded and her chin crinkled. "The nerve of that big gorilla," she said. "Busting in on me like that."

"He was just doing his job. Mrs. Harrison sent him?"

Her chin crinkled some more and her brow furrowed; the whole avoid-wrinkles regimen was out the window this morning. "She must have. The nasty bitch."

Ignoring this touching sentiment for the widow of her late benefactor, I said, "So, then, Mrs. Harrison must have known about you."

"She knows about me. She's not an idiot. She's a fat, pampered bitch, but not an idiot." Her face turned toward mine. "So, you *know* that goon of hers, this Morelli creature?"

"Morella. Hank Morella. Sure."

"What's that Neanderthal's story, anyway?"

That Neanderthal's story was a fairly interesting one, and I shared it with her. Henry Morella had ties back to Frank Calabria, supposedly a cousin of one of Calabria's top lieutenants, who requested of the mob boss that something nonviolent and noncriminal be found for his sister's boy. And Morella *was* just a "boy," back then, specifically a glorified office boy, a kid who served as Donny's chief gopher.

"When I mentioned the other day," I said to her, as she listened and sipped coffee, "that Donny began in the sleaze racket, you seemed in the dark."

She nodded. "All I ever knew was he and Louie were in the printing business. The only publishing I heard about was Yiddish newspapers in the late '20s, early '30s."

"Before your time," I said with a shrug. "Hell, before *my* time. They published a line of magazines that were pretty risque for back then . . . a lot of them had 'Saucy' or 'Spicy' in the titles."

Her eyes tightened; she was back to the nonwrinkling expressiveness I'd grown to know and love. "But they weren't . . . pornographic or anything . . ."

"Not quite. The trade name for 'em was 'smooshes'—pulp fiction magazines with a heavy dollop of sex, and particularly racy covers and illustrations. Some of the artists working at Americana today, doing patriotic funny books for kiddies, were responsible for that raunchy stuff. Donny also did showbiz mags with leg art of starlets and showgirls and strippers; also 'art' magazines with models who were so very artistic, they would even pose with their shirts off."

She seemed mildly appalled. "*Wonder Guy* Donny was involved with that kind of trash?"

Didn't have the heart to remind her what her role in *Wonder Guy* Donny's life had been.

I flipped a hand. "That's where the heroes of American kids everywhere were born—out of the muck of mags like *Spicy Models*. But I can't get too indignant, considering both my mother and my two stepmothers appeared in those very pages."

Her eyes sparkled and she laughed as she said, "Really? Oh, that's wonderful."

"You seem to be over the outrage of Donny publishing pornography."

She made herself stop laughing. "I'm sorry. It just . . . struck my funny bone is all. But where does Morelli come in?"

"Morella. Well, Donny was trying to test the limits, you know—really see what he could get away with? So he published an un-airbrushed photo of a lovely lass in an issue of *Saucy Sweeties* . . ."

"What do you mean . . . un-airbrushed?"

"I mean, an untouched-up frontal view that revealed the blonde was a brunette."

Honey covered her mouth with a red-nailed hand; those nails were starting to need some touch-up, themselves. She was amused and horrified, always an interesting combination.

"So," I went on, "Donny got indicted for publishing obscene materials . . ."

"No!"

"Yes. And the DA's office was looking at jail time."

She shook her head, certain I was fantasizing or maybe hallucinating. "Donny never did a day in jail in his life!"

"No he didn't . . . but Hank Morella did. Hank took full responsibility for that clear and yet fuzzy photo."

Her eyes were bigger than Betty Boop's. "Why on earth would he do that?"

"Well, Hank was listed as an editor on the masthead of several of Donny and Louie's mags. He did no editing, of course, but the title helped justify the decent paycheck the kid earned, as a favor to silent-partner Calabria. Anyway, Donny retroactively anointed Hank the real editor of *Saucy Sweeties*, and Hank took the full blame, saying he'd sneaked in the questionable photo without Donny or Louie's knowledge."

Slowly shaking her head, she said, "I still don't understand why Morelli . . . Morella . . . would *do* that?"

"He's what we call in the detective business a fall guy, Honey. He took the heat off Donny. Served six months, and emerged to a lifetime position as Donny's driver. Which is why he's on Americana's payroll."

Her smile was as skeptical as it was pretty. "You're making all of this up."

"If I had that good an imagination," I said, "I'd be *drawing* comic strips, not helping syndicate 'em."

I rose, yawned, excused myself and said, "I need to take my leave, Miss Daily. All play and no work makes Jack a dull boy. But you whip up a mean omelet, and I would love to be invited back."

A vision in white and pink and blonde, she stood and, holding on to one of my arms with both of hers, walked me toward the foyer and said, "Consider yourself the proud bearer of an open invitation. Only next time, call first. I must have looked a mess last night."

"Frightening," I said, and shivered.

We were at the door now.

"I bet you get slapped a lot," she said.

"It has happened."

I kissed her, and took my leave, glancing back to catch her wicked little smile and sweet little girl wave before the door closed.

She said nothing, and yet I could still hear her voice saying, *I like you. You're silly.*

And I could still remember how poorly Sylvester the Cat had fared in that cartoon . . .

To refer to what the Waldorf offered a guy in need of a haircut and shave as a barbershop would be like calling the Radio City Music Hall a movie house. I left my fedora at the hatcheck window and ambled into the gleaming marble-and-chrome chamber, rows of black-padded porcelain chairs at left and right, attended by a white-uniformed army of barbers, mirrors on facing walls making an infinity cut of this world of scissors and hair tonic and scalp massages.

Down toward the left—past where the right wall of chairs halted to make way for manicure booths—waited one empty chair.

I knew that chair was empty for a reason, that reason being that Frank Calabria was seated in the one next to it. Calabria's was the final chair near the back wall and its bench meant for half a dozen waiting customers. Right now that bench was taken up by only two individuals, the same two I'd seen last night in the hotel lobby: Calabria's bagman Big Jim and the pockmarked hood with the loose-fitting suitcoat that failed to hide the obvious artillery.

Above the seated bodyguards, hanging off a cabinet knob like a precious painting on a museum wall, was the coat of a gray pinstriped suit, with a darker gray fedora hanging on the knob next to it. The jacket represented maybe two hundred bucks out of the total price of the suit it belonged to, while the black-banded fedora probably went for a meager hundred and fifty clams, give or take a pearl.

Once Frank Calabria's lawyer had told him to stop wearing $350 suits to court; Calabria had informed said lawyer that he'd rather do time than wear cheap threads.

I ignored the counter where the barbershop version of a maitre d' told you how long the wait was—assuming you were going to be allowed in—and strode to that empty chair and planted myself in it.

This got the attention of all kinds of people, though Calabria himself was under a hot towel and white cape. His barber, a little gray-haired, round-faced, black-mustached character, turned whiter than his smock and gave me the kind of look Dracula must get a lot.

The pockmarked threat started up off the bench, but ferret-faced Big Jim held him back, smiling at me (I guess you'd call what those misshapen yellow pegs added up to a smile) and whispering to his fellow bodyguard.

A skinny barber—black hair, also mustached—came up and began telling me this chair wasn't available while at the same time Big Jim informed the face under the pile of steaming towel that Jack Starr was here. Calabria interrupted both men, staying under the towel, his voice muffled but easy to make out.

"Jack! You need a haircut?"

I said, "Yeah, Frank, and a shave. You mind? Chair was open."

From under the towel, without knowing who he was addressing exactly, he said, "Give this kid a shave and a haircut, and put it on my tab! Kid's a Silver Star winner, for Christ's sake!"

When you've known somebody a long time, they can get away with calling you a kid. And when they're Frank Calabria, they can call you anything they want.

The skinny barber washed my hair before he started cutting, by which time Calabria was in the middle of his shave. Over against the wall, the two seated bodyguards watched me like I was Old Faithful and might erupt any minute. Big Jim had a *Police Gazette* on his lap, the pockmarked one *Ring*, the boxing mag.

My barber, whose name tag said MARIO, started trimming without asking me for instructions. I decided not to spook him any further with such trifles as how I wanted my hair cut. I'd be lucky to make it out of Mario's chair with both ears.

Calabria's barber, the small round-faced gray-haired one (name tag: TONY), was not in the least nervous. My presence had been adjusted to. Calabria was, obviously, a regular customer. And Calabria would require and expect a steady hand.

Fifty-five maybe, Calabria was a big man—not tall, probably only five-eight or -nine, but wide-shouldered and massive without much apparent fat. He had a lumpy face that somehow arrived at something not unattractive, his widow's-peaked hair on the blondish side with white coming in unobtrusively. He was like the best-looking iguana you ever saw.

"So a friend of ours died," Calabria said.

Tony's razor was expertly removing lather and whiskers.

Over the snip, snip, snip of Mario's scissors, I said, "You mean, a friend of yours and mine, Frank? . . . Or a friend of the family?"

And he knew what "family" I meant.

Calabria laughed, but his face remained immobile—he had a blade at his throat, after all. "How old were you when I first saw you, kid?"

"I don't know, Frank. Was it that time the major took me out to Belmont?"

"Maybe it was, yeah. Six? Seven?"

"Eight, probably. I don't think the major would've taken a six- or seven-year-old to a racetrack."

"Eight, say," Calabria said. "And you was a wiseass even then."

"Some things you never grow out of."

With mirrors fore and aft, countless eyes around the shop were sneaking peeks, pretending not to. Scissors sang a metallic song, the nasal twang of manicurists providing a chorus, while scalp massage machines made like an orchestra of electric kazoos.

"I don't scare you, do I, kid, like I do some of these panty-waists."

"Frank, I just try not to do anything to make you want to scare me."

"Ha. You come walkin' in here like you own the place. Come over and sit down right next to me in a chair that's empty on purpose."

"I needed a shave."

"And you wanted to talk to me, right, kid?"

"Why, sure—didn't you ever want to kill two birds with one stone, Frank?"

My barber and Calabria's barber were looking at each other bug-eyed, wondering if they were about to share a crossfire. But there was nothing to worry about. The major had loved Frank

Calabria, and Frank Calabria had loved the major, and I was the major's kid.

Tony was toweling off Calabria's remaining lather when the mob boss finally glanced at me. "You *do* need a shave, kid."

"Well, I spent the night with a beautiful woman up in her tower suite. You oughta try that sometime, Frank. Clears the sinuses."

He laughed, this time letting his face in on the action. Tony was applying a creamy film to Calabria's cheeks, preparing to take one more close pass on his rocky puss with that gleaming razor.

"I saw your fellas in the lobby," I said, "on my way up, yesterday evening. Do they just sit there all night and wait till you need a shave?"

The two bodyguards were glaring at me. And, by the way, they both could have used shaves themselves.

"Something like that, kid," Calabria said. "They kinda take turns sleeping."

"And yet the hotel management doesn't toss them out for loitering."

"They got a friend in a high place."

Up a Waldorf Tower with his mistress.

I asked, "Did they spot an old friend of yours, going up?"

With a frown on that iguana pan of his, Calabria was watching me in the mirror opposite; but the width of the shop was such that this didn't provide much of a view—strictly long shots, no close-ups, in the movie playing in the mirror.

"*What* old friend, kid?"

"Hank Morella."

"Oh, little Hank! No, we didn't see him go up. When was this?"

"Half an hour ago, more or less."

"No, no, kid, we was already in here. Older a guy gets, longer it takes to spruce him up. Where was Hank off to?"

"Picking up Donny's things from the former love nest. Two suitcases worth."

Still trying to watch me in that too-distant mirror, Calabria asked, "Is that where *you* were, kid? Honey Daily's suite? You don't waste any time. Hell, neither does she."

"Frank, I don't kiss and tell. But I will admit I've spoken to Miss Daily recently."

"What about did you speak to her?"

"Donny's murder."

Calabria told his barber to back off a second, and gazed over at me. "Yeah, I heard the cops think it's a killing. And I would dearly love to see whoever done that to Donny get his head handed to him. But why is it your business, kid?"

"Those two naive chumps behind *Wonder Guy*," I said, "are looking like the prime suspects. And we do business with those very chumps, *and* with Americana, so Maggie wants this thing cracked fast."

His eyes slitted as they studied me. "Don't you think the homicide boys are up to the job?"

"Do they know who to talk to? Could some city flatfoot get you to talk so free and easy, like I'm doing?"

He laughed loud enough to tempt other patrons to look at him, though they didn't, or anyway pretended not to, and he motioned to Tony to start back in on the shave.

"Kid, I will help you if I can. In fact, if you need anything, just say so."

"Then you and Donny were pals till the end?"

"Who *says* we weren't?"

"Rumor has it Donny, and Louie Cohn for that matter, have forgotten their roots, and who got them started. Have neglected old friends and turned their noses up at longtime relationships, personal and business. Rumor has it."

Scissors sang, manicurists twanged.

"Donny and Louie," Calabria said finally, "sell comic books to children. Their business interests and mine do not have no common ground no more."

Which was horse hockey—the publishing business could supply a man like Frank Calabria with various avenues of distribution for a variety of products, as well as provide fronts for laundering gambling and drug money.

But even the major's son couldn't get away with disagreeing with Frank Calabria on such a point.

"Will I see you at the funeral this afternoon, Frank?"

". . . I got business conflicts."

For many years, Donny and Louie and, for a time, my father had been Calabria's Jewish *paisans*. After Prohibition ended, Calabria needed new rackets, and the two men who would later sell *Wonder Guy* to ten-year-olds of all ages had helped Calabria find them. Their publishing interests, the girlies and smooshes, were sold in cigar stores and in drugstores and on newsstands, and the same distribution system that legally delivered magazines could also provide the sub rosa services attached to the numbers game, illegal bookmaking and slot machines.

Mario was lathering me up now, and Tony swept the cape away and began giving Calabria the whisk-broom treatment. The gangster's tie was a striped silk of alternating shades of gray, and cost more than the average New Yorker's weekly rent.

I watched as the mob leader descended from the barber-chair throne, got whisked off some more, then dug into his pocket and removed a fat bankroll from which he peeled two twenties for his barber, who took it, bowed, thanked him profusely, and retreated.

The pockmarked guy helped Calabria into his suitcoat, and Big Jim handed him his fedora. Calabria held a hand up to them, indicating they should stay put for a moment, and walked over to me. He took a moment to regally don the hat, then stood right in front of me, a commanding figure, freshly barbered and shaved, looking and smelling like a million legal bucks. He had dark blue eyes with a lot of eyelash, almost feminine, although the unblinking deadness of them was strictly masculine.

Almost whispering, he said, "I would like to go to that funeral. Nobody told me I couldn't. But I know my attending could be seen as not a positive thing. And I wouldn't never do that to the grieving widow."

My barber, upon Calabria approaching, had stopped in mid-shave, so I could risk a nod.

Calabria leaned in so close I could smell the aftershave tonic. Rosewater.

"Kid," he asked in a near whisper, "do you think you know who did this to Donny?"

"Not yet." I was keeping my voice down, too.

"But you will?"

"I think so. This homicide dick, Chandler, isn't stupid, but you should still put your money on me."

"I'm willing to, kid."

". . . Pardon?"

His eyes narrowed and his smile widened. Still in that conspiratorial near-whisper, he asked, "What would you say to ten grand for finding Donny's killer?"

"I'd say . . . hello."

He raised a palm, as if half surrendering. "I mean, I understand you already have a client, and I don't wish to impugn your ethics . . ."

"Impugn away, Frank. I don't see any conflict of interest here."

Calabria smiled a deceptively mild-mannered smile. "If I was involved, in this murder? There would be."

I shrugged. "Then give me the full ten grand up front, which protects me in such a case."

He chuckled, shook his head, then chuckled some more. "The major would be proud of you, kid. You got a streak of hustle in you, and more guts than sense. You want me to have the check messengered over?"

"Naw, just stick it in the mail. Nice doing business with you, Frank."

He nodded, his expression avuncular. "Keep in touch, kid. You need anything, just let me know. You have the private number, right?"

"Right," I said.

Calabria and his entourage trooped out, the two bodyguards apparently unsure whether to nod respectfully or glare at me, and hedged their bet by doing neither.

After the haircut and shave, which Calabria had paid for (I tipped the guy five bucks for preserving both ears), I found my way to a bank of phone booths in the lobby. I spent a nickel and Bryce put me on with Maggie.

"Where are you?" she asked, her concern edged with irritation. "I called downstairs to see if you'd have breakfast with me, but got no answer."

"I'm at the Waldorf," I said. "I had breakfast in Honey Daily's suite. Cooked it for me herself."

". . . Are you planning to sleep with all the suspects?"

"No, I thought I'd take the women, and you could start with Spiegel and Shulman."

I could almost hear her shudder over the line.

"Anything interesting to report?" she asked. "Besides your love life?"

I filled her in about Honey's take on Rod Krane and Louis Cohn and Will Hander as suspects, as well as Hank Morella dropping by for Donny's things. And finished up with my close shave with Calabria and company.

"You took him on as a client?" she asked. "Since when are you taking on clients?"

"Since I can pick up an easy ten grand and get Frank Calabria's cooperation."

"You think we'll need it?"

"Maggie, I don't know. I really don't. But it's nice to know Calabria will take my calls. Donny came out of the rackets, and who can say his murder isn't connected?"

"More hoodlums die by violence," Maggie said philosophically, "than editors or publishers."

"Yeah, and more hoodlums die by violence in Americana comic books than in real life. You haven't changed your mind about attending the funeral, have you?"

"No. No, that's all yours."

"You don't think less of me, do you?"

"For what, Jack?"

"My slumber party with Donny's girlfriend."

"That's right, Jack," one of the world's most famous striptease artists said, "I'm shocked by the very notion of sex. I hope you watched those movies about venereal disease when you were in the army."

"Why, which ones did you star in?"

I could hear her trying not to laugh at that, then she said, "You've got the whole morning left—next stop?"

"Americana Comics," I said. "That whoosh you're about to hear is me flying over there."

The morning was overcast and cool, and the few blocks from the Waldorf over to the editorial offices of Americana Comics on Lexington Avenue made for a pleasant, even bracing walk. The lack of July heat made Manhattan pedestrians less surly than the norm, and I only got sworn at three times and wasn't spit upon at all. I still would rather have had time to stop at my digs for a shower, but the fresh shave and haircut made me feel human enough to venture into the world. Donny's funeral would kill the afternoon, so I needed to squeeze some life out of the hours available.

The Americana waiting room on the fourth floor of the Dixon Building on Lexington Avenue might have been any austerely businesslike reception area but for one thing: on the wood-paneled wall behind a good-looking blonde receptionist loomed a huge gold-framed portrait . . . not of the founder of the company (except perhaps figuratively), rather of a muscular figure in a flapping blue cape and red muscleman tights with a white W on his expansive chest, and blue boots. Fists at his waist, smiling confidently, chin up, Wonder Guy stood on an outcropping of rock, poised against a blue sky streaked by white clouds, with a Manhattan skyline faintly discernible at a distant horizon.

The waiting room had half a dozen chairs at left and right, with end tables providing the latest news magazines but no comic books—Americana's product was for kids, but its offices were for the grown-ups. Closed doors on either side of the reception desk were labeled EDITORIAL and PRODUCTION, respectively.

The blonde guarding the gate wore black-rimmed glasses, as if to mask her beauty—the tactic might have worked for mild-mannered radio reporter Ron Benson, Wonder Guy's secret identity, but this doll in the well-filled white blouse with lace-filled keyhole neckline needed a better disguise.

She knew me enough to say, "Good morning, Mr. Starr," though I didn't remember her name and no nameplate on her desk was there to remind me. I did, however, recall how nice her legs were, having seen her up and out from behind that desk a few times.

And before you label me a shameless ogler of feminine pulchritude, let me defend myself by saying all the distaff staffers at Americana were notoriously good-looking, the best legs and fullest busts on display in any single Manhattan office.

This was yet another part of Donny Harrison's enduring legacy.

Even Wonder Guy seemed to have a certain leer going in that

great big painting. Of course, the portrait—the accomplished oil technique of which was something that would have eluded cartoonist Moe Shulman—was the work of an artist who used to provide raunchy covers to Donny's old sexy pulp magazines.

Somehow that said it all—that the signature painting of the red-white-and-blue hero of America's youth had been executed by a guy who more commonly depicted slobbering males (mad scientists, cannibals, Red Indians) in the process of ripping the remaining shreds of clothing off tied-up nubile maidens.

"Isn't it terrible about Mr. Harrison?" the receptionist said, big brown eyes behind the glasses staring up at me with unblinking insincerity.

"A shame," I said. "How's the office holding up?"

"We're all too busy to be sad," she said, even though none of the waiting room chairs was occupied, and her desk—but for an appointment book, intercom box and blotter—was bare as a newborn's behind. "We have to get a whole day's work done by noon."

"Ah. The funeral."

"Yes." Then she brightened. "We're closing early!"

"Are you going?"

"Uh, no. None of us girls are. We were talking and some of us were planning to, but it's funny . . . Mr. Cohn was quite insistent that this was only for close family and friends."

She seemed quite befuddled by this exclusion. I, on the other hand, grasped immediately why a full row of busty, leggy secretaries might not be welcome by, say, Mrs. Harrison at her beloved husband's service. Too bad, since I did have to attend (close friend), and it would have passed the time trying to guess which of the Americana girls Donny had merely pinched, and which he'd bent over a desk for some corporate punishment.

"Speaking of Mr. Cohn," I said, "I'd like to see him."

"I think he's on an important long-distance call, Mr. Starr. But he should be done within half an hour. Would you care to wait?"

"How about Sy Mortimer? Is he in?"

"He is. Would you like me to buzz him?"

"Yes."

She did, and Sy would see me—seventh office on the right.

Before I headed through the EDITORIAL door, however, I said to her, "I'm afraid I've forgotten your name."

"Daisy."

"Daisy, would you be sure to let Mr. Cohn know that I'm here, and that I'd like to see him?"

"Certainly, Mr. Starr. Should I ring you in Mr. Mortimer's office, when Mr. Cohn is available?"

"Would you?"

The EDITORIAL and PRODUCTION doors opened onto the same hallway, but to the right the hall emptied out into a big bullpen of artists. Death comes to us all, but life and commerce go on, as even now a dozen cartoonists, behind a battery of drawing boards, were at work on comic-book pages under a cloud of tobacco smoke. Some of these men in their twenties and thirties—shirtsleeves rolled up, ties loosened—would be penciling pages, others inking them, still more doing lettering, both the dialogue balloons and the explosive sound effects—BAM!, POW!, ZAP!, WHAM!

The smoky chamber was oddly joyless, and at least as silent as Donny Harrison's funeral would be, each artist deep in his work, the only sounds the soft dissonant symphony of scratching pen tips and rubbing of pencil lead and rubber eraser against the tooth of bristol board, with an occasional grunt or groan providing percussion.

Attitudes toward their late publisher would be mixed among these men (female cartoonists were rare if not unknown in the comic-book business), as Donny had been renowned for paying freelancers well for the initial work, but retaining all rights.

And these men were freelancers, not employees, given space to work in out of the generosity of Americana's heart, but without the benefits a company employee might expect or at least lobby for.

None of these fellows were creators of properties; you would rarely if ever find Rod Krane or Moe Shulman here (they had their own studios). This was the anonymous army of funny-book artists who drew various second-string superheroes and backup features and covers and occasionally *Wonder Guy* and *Batwing* stories, when the Krane and Shulman crews were unable to fill the need. Wonder Guy, after all, appeared in his own book as well as *Active Comics* and *World's Strongest Heroes*; Batwing appeared in his own book, and *Detection Comics* as well as *World's Strongest*.

Hundreds of pages a month had to be churned out to keep all that newsprint chugging along in four colors, to keep kids of all ages trading in their dimes for comic books.

A few faces looked up at me as I took in this factory of creativity, and the ones that recognized me and nodded, I nodded back at.

Then I headed left, down the carpeted hall. At right were editors' offices—wood-and-glass fronted, providing no privacy (but evidence to bosses Donny and Louis that their people were hard at work). Some offices had double occupancy, but most were solo, the desks big and wooden and formidable, providing plenty of space for the oversize comic-page original art the editors would have to deal with.

Every single office had the cluttered look of ongoing, even frantic work, typical in a deadline-driven business like the comics. Cover proofs, some in black-and-white, others watercolored as printer's guides, plus full-color printer's proofs, were tacked on bulletin boards and sometimes Scotch-taped to walls; file cabinets were piled with papers and portfolios and original art and printed comic books.

At left I initially passed a long, narrow glass-and-wood fronted office filled with smaller wooden desks with typing stands. This was the secretarial pool, and a group of lovely young women who rivaled the Copacabana chorus line were machine-gunning along on their Smith Coronas.

The next room on the left was an open break area, half a dozen tables with two walls filled by counters and cupboards with a coffeemaker and all the trimmings. The other wall was home to a humming Coca-Cola machine and a refrigerator. Nobody was on break, so I slipped in and had a look inside the fridge.

Wax-wrapped sandwiches, some small individual bottles of milk and a few candy bars were about it—no insulin vials, although this was undoubtedly where Donny had kept them . . . meaning dozens of people at Americana had easy access to same.

Back in the hall, along the left wall—on the other side of which was the boardroom—were lined framed one-sheet posters of movie productions of Americana properties: the Republic *Wonder Guy* and *Batwing* serials, several of the *Wonder Guy* animated cartoons from MGM. A few industry magazine advertisements for the *Wonder Guy* radio show were also on display, and another frame showed off *Wonder Guy* and *Batwing* candy bar wrappers.

Finally I arrived at managing editor Sy Mortimer's space, the last of the glass/wood-fronted offices, the next two—Donny Harrison's and Louis Cohn's—being larger and private. Donny, in particular, had not wanted to be disturbed while he was working, perhaps when he was giving dictation to one of those showgirl-worthy secretaries.

Sy Mortimer, ironically, had been a part of the circle of science-fiction fans in the '30s that had included Harry Spiegel and Moe Shulman. Though Mortimer was from the Bronx and the boys from Des Moines, they had met through the mail and joined forces in the so-called fanzines that they self-published, a form invented by Harry Spiegel—cartoons and book and movie reviews and science fiction created by teenaged enthusiasts for others like them.

Mortimer had parlayed this amateur work into editing pulp magazines for Donny Harrison, then became a literary agent for science-fiction writers he'd met as a fan and editor, and at the same time began writing comic-book scripts for Americana, creating two of their most unmemorable superheroes, the Blue Barracuda and the Red Archer.

Mortimer's desk was as work-laden as any of the others, and glass-and-wood wall or not, the plump, round-faced, bald-on-top editor in shirtsleeves and loosened *Wonder Guy* tie, hunkered over a big piece of comic art with a blue pencil in his fist, didn't spot me till I knocked. Then he brightened as if we were old buddies—we really weren't, though we knew each other to speak to—and waved me on in, grinning.

"Morning, Sy," I said. "Thanks for seeing me. I know this has to be a hard day for you."

He wiped the grin off and worked up a solemn expression. "Yes, Jack, it really is." He had a big, booming voice that damn near made the window glass rattle. He gesticulated a lot and, despite his unimpressive appearance, had a commanding manner. "But work is a solace. And Donny would've wanted us to stay in the saddle."

"With such attractive female help as additional solace," I said, and smiled, "I'm sure he would want you to . . . stay in the saddle. Mind if I sit?"

His expression curdled as he decided whether to acknowledge my sarcasm or not. "No. No, please do, Jack. But I do have several issues to get out to the printers today, and an abbreviated time span to do it in—"

I took the visitor's chair opposite him, and rested an ankle on a knee. "Funny you should say that, 'cause somebody must've had an issue with Donny, too . . . and abbreviated *his* time span . . . right?"

"Right." He shook his head, tossed the blue pencil on the artwork, an *Amazonia* page rife with underclad women running and jumping. "I thought it was a heart attack or something, or maybe Donny just got weak-headed from his condition and all, and passed out on that knife."

"So did I."

His eyebrows rose—they had plenty of room. "Yes, and thank God that's how it wound up in the papers—a weird accident."

"Well, they'll get the real story sooner or later, Sy, don't you think?"

He shrugged. "I don't know. I hope they don't. With Louis's connections, who knows? Maybe the cops'll keep it under wraps. That captain who dropped around, first thing this morning, he seemed okay enough."

"He collected Donny's insulin, right?"

"Right." Mortimer shifted in his seat, sat forward. "What's your interest in this, Jack? I mean, no offense, I get that Americana and the Starr Syndicate do business. But I never had the feeling that Donny Harrison was your favorite person in the world."

"He wasn't. The major was fond of him, though."

Sy nodded; the overhead florescent lights, buzzing like mosquitoes, reflected on his bald pate. "A lot of people were fond of Donny, me included. He could be a hell of a lot of fun—nobody ever had a better way with the ol' rack jobbers out in the hinterlands."

"Cigars and booze and broads make a lot of friends."

He pawed the air. "You make it sound cheap and sleazy. He was a fun-loving guy who liked people and people liked him. Donny would take doughnuts and coffee to the truckers loading up bundles of comics. He would—"

"Treat you like crap, Sy?"

That froze him. The fat little man with the booming big voice was reduced to whispering: "Why . . . why do you say that?"

"Because I've seen it. He belittled you, Sy. He made fun of you and made your life miserable, piling your desk with more work than Scrooge gave Marley."

He leaned forward, pressing his presence on me. "Donny was no goddamn Scrooge!"

I kept my tone casual. "No. He paid you generously, and after you ate a fifty-pound bag of his fertilizer—or was it a one-hundred-pound bag? He rewarded your hard work with this position. How's it going, incidentally?"

Mortimer had been managing editor for less than a year.

He swallowed, and began blinking. "Very well. Great. Wonderful. Why?"

"Because I understand Americana sales have dropped a third, since the end of the war."

His shrug was twice as elaborate as necessary. "Market's glutted. We're still the top of the superhero heap."

"What about Spiggot Publications and *Marvel Man*?"

He sat back and batted the air. "We still outsell them overall and, anyway, Louie's taking care of that."

"With the plagiarism lawsuit."

"Right." He came forward again. "What are we talking about, anyway, Jack? Why are you so down on everything and everybody? You're asking more questions than that cop."

"That cop doesn't know what questions to ask. He's not on the inside of this business like I am."

His eyes narrowed. "So . . . what's your interest in this awful tragedy? How does it affect Starr?"

"We syndicate the *Wonder Guy* and *Batwing* strips, and Spiegel and Shulman are both suspects, and for that matter so is Rod Krane."

He laughed loud, a big forced laugh that probably didn't even convince him. "Those pipsqueaks Harry and Moe, murder somebody? That's dumber than anything we ever published. And Krane had no reason to want Donny out of the way—he's got a much better contract than the boys, and if he has any complaints about Americana, I never heard 'em."

"Nonetheless, I'm looking into the murder."

He gestured to himself with both hands, and acted astounded. "So, what? *I'm* a suspect now?"

"Why, do you have a motive?"

His face turned white. "Don't be an ass."

Now I sat forward. "*Do* you have a motive, Sy? When I go asking around, what am I going to hear about you and Donny that you wish I wouldn't?"

He swallowed and tried to smile, but if that sick thing was a smile, I never saw one. "If . . . if there was some disagreement or something, why would I tell you about it?"

I shrugged. "So I hear it here first. So any false accusations anybody makes will have the legs cut out from under them, by you telling me the true facts."

"Well . . . we did get into it last week, I suppose, Donny and me. But that was just a business blowup, kind that happens, time to time."

"What sort of business blowup?"

The sick supposed grin again. "I guess you know the boys . . . Harry and Moe . . . their contract comes up soon."

"Right."

"And . . . and they really don't have a leg to stand on. The deal they made as kids may be lousy, but it's legal."

"So some say."

He put a hand on his endless forehead, like he was taking his own temperature. "Well . . . I did something that maybe, might have, you know, given them ammunition, the boys."

"Which is?"

He let out a long sigh and looked toward me but not at me, glazed. "Before I was editor here, Harry submitted an idea for a kid version of *Wonder Guy*—all about Wonder Guy's childhood in Littleburg as a kid, Ron Benson growing up on a farm, dealing with his powers and having to keep them a secret. *Wonder Boy*."

"Sure. That came out early this year, right? Very successful."

He was sweating. The air-conditioning in here was fine, but he was beading up like crazy. "Yes . . . but Donny rejected the idea, back in '42 when Harry first proposed it. Only . . . only I ran across it in the files, and thought it had potential, and, hell, it was Harry and Moe I gave it to, to produce, wasn't it? Their studio is doing it."

"Then what's the problem?"

"Problem is . . . we published it without a new contract. I figured it was just an extension of *Wonder Guy*. A spin-off, like with *The Fibber McGee and Molly Show*, when they gave the Gildersleeve character his own radio program."

"Sure. They did the same thing with Beulah the maid."

He sat so far forward I could smell his breath, which was no treat. "But then Donny and Louis came in and . . . I'm being straight with you, Jack. You keep this to yourself."

"Sure, Sy."

"Anyway . . . Donny and Louie tore me a great big gaping new one over this . . . this 'gaffe,' they called it. Harry and Moe claim *Wonder Boy* is a new, separate property—and Americana having turned it down, only to publish it without permission, further fuels the fire. They're gonna use this to club us with, in the new negotiation."

"And Louis and Donny really let you have it, huh?"

He got a handkerchief from his pocket and mopped his brow. "Donny did. You know how Louis is—cold and quiet, but I got the point; and if I didn't, Donny hammered it home. He . . . he'd just started speaking to me again, before . . . before he died."

"Sy, I'm going to ask you a personal question. I understand if you take a pass on answering."

"What?"

"You were friendly with Harry and Moe back when you were kids—you weren't from the same part of the country, but you were part of the same loosely organized group of science-fiction fans. You knew each other. Wrote letters, contributed to each other's amateur publications."

His eyes tightened as he tried to see where this was going. "Sure. We even met a few times. I went west and they came east."

"What I want to ask is this, Sy—if the boys were friends of yours, why haven't you been able to patch this up? Convince

135

Donny and Louie to give their star performers a break, and make Harry and Moe behave themselves and be professionals? Grown-ups?"

Sy had already started shaking his head halfway through that. "Jack, the problem is, the boys came up with a great idea, back in Des Moines a million years ago . . . but they don't have what it takes to keep *Wonder Guy* going, keep it current and vital."

"How so? The strip we syndicate seems fine."

"The strip is good," he said, nodding. "Of course, I'll lay odds Harry's having the writing ghosted, and that artwork is surely not Moe's—poor bastard is half blind, or haven't you noticed those Coke bottles he wears?"

I folded my arms. "What do you care who's doing the work, as long as it's professional?"

"Harry is doing most of the comic-book writing himself, Jack. And he's doing it poorly—the same, silly lighthearted stuff he did before and during the war. Kid stuff. Do you know how strong our sales were on military bases? *Wonder Guy* went through the roof at the PXs."

"Wasn't *that* the same silly, lighthearted stuff?"

"Right, and a perfect reminder of back home. But the war is over, and the vets who aren't wounded or shellshocked saw plenty of their buddies get that way."

"Sy, I'm not following."

He pointed at me like Uncle Whiskers recruiting. "Follow this, Jack—the GIs learned to read and like comic books. Cheap, portable entertainment they could roll up and stick in a back pocket or in a knapsack, and throw away when they were done.

They were eighteen, nineteen years old, these kids. Now they're in their twenties, heading toward thirty. What this business has to do is hang on to those readers. We can survive this downswing by drawing in the kids and keeping them, but keeping the older readers, too."

"Sure, like these romance and western and crime comics that are coming out." I shrugged. "But what does this have to do with Harry Spiegel?"

Sy shook his head and tried a different smile, a sad one, and this one took. "His stuff only works on the kid level, Jack. You know, I worked for a time as an agent—I was the very first science-fiction literary agent, did you know that?"

"Yes."

He pointed at himself with two thumbs. "And I'm bringing in good talent, top talent, real science-fiction writers who can breathe some life into *Wonder Guy*. The truth is, we just don't need Harry Spiegel anymore . . . and we sure don't need a blind cartoonist like Moe Shulman."

"Donny agreed with you on this approach?"

And *this* smile I really believed, because it was a sneer. "Why do you think he made me managing editor?"

"Oh, I don't know—your compassion and humanity?"

That stopped him for a second, long enough for his intercom to buzz.

Daisy's voice said, "*Mr. Cohn will see Mr. Starr now, Mr. Mortimer. In the boardroom.*"

I stood. "Thanks for the time, Sy."

He looked up at me and for once his expression struck me as

earnest. "I loved Donny. We'd had a business argument, but nothing to kill anybody over. You seem to have a low opinion of me, Jack, and, well, that's your prerogative. But I do want Donny's murder solved, and if I can help, you know where to find me."

"Thanks." At the doorway, I stopped and threw a question at him: "Did you know about Donny's diabetes, by the way?"

He blinked. "Of course."

"And that insulin that Captain Chandler collected . . . was it well known here at Americana that that was Donny's medication?"

"Everybody knew."

"Do you happen to know whether Donny took his medication here, Thursday afternoon, or at Miss Daily's suite?"

"I have no idea."

"Okay. Thanks, Sy. See you at the funeral."

The boardroom door was just down the hall, toward the end near the fire exit, and across from Louis Cohn's office. I went in and found Cohn, in a black suit and black tie (ready for the funeral), seated down at the head of the long mahogany table.

The dark-paneled room was largely unadorned, but on the wall behind the chairman's chair—in an echo of the waiting room and its Wonder Guy portrait—hung a large formal portrait of Donny Harrison, a smiling head-and-shoulders shot in blue business suit and red tie, no hands on hips and flapping cape. But I do believe it was done by the same artist as the waiting-room Wonder Guy (and dozens of lurid pulp covers).

"What brings you around, Jack?" Cohn asked. He had a higher-pitched voice than Sy Mortimer, but the big room and all that wood lent it resonance. He was sitting back in his padded leather chair, hands folded over a small paunch—even a thin guy like Louie, in his midfifties, carried a little extra weight, maybe to balance the thinning of his swept-back, widow's-peaked black hair.

I shrugged and, fedora in hand, walked down to him. "Paying my respects," I said, with a nod toward the looming portrait.

"That's what funerals are for," Cohn said. He had a neat trick of sneering without making his mustache twitch.

"Mind if I sit?"

"And if I did mind?" His expression was blank, though the dark eyes conveyed a coldness matched by his tone; he had a smooth face, like a baby, or like an adult who'd managed not to feel much of anything in five decades plus.

I sat. Tossed my fedora on the table. "You seem to be bearing up under the strain."

He was rocking ever so gently. "You never liked Donny, and you never liked me. Even as a boy. But your father was a good man, and he liked us both."

"Sorry to be a party pooper."

The dark eyes flashed. "I'll ask again. Why are you here, Jack? This is a short workday for us, and do I have to tell you a difficult one?"

"Yeah, I can see how you're working at holding your emotions in, losing your best friend like this."

He sighed irritably. "Donny was not my best friend. He was a business partner, and a valued one. We made a good team. We were never friendly outside of work, or work-related events."

To call this guy a cold fish was to insult a dead carp.

"Louie, I'm looking into the murder."

That seemed to get his attention; his head cocked sideways like the RCA Victor dog, and he made a sound deep in his throat that was damn near a growl.

But what he said was, "That's idiotic. What are you supposed to be, a detective?"

"Actually, yes. You're aware I'm licensed in this state?"

Again he sneered and the mustache remained horizontal; maybe it was painted on. "To do your stepmother's troubleshooting and dirty work, you are. This is a police matter. In fact, Captain Chandler has already been here and spoken to me. He's seems competent."

"He is."

"Then why this ridiculous exercise in futility?"

I imitated his posture, folding my hands over my stomach, which was flat, but what the hell. "If you're referring to my efforts to clear up Donny's murder, it was as much Maggie Starr's idea as mine. I know the people, and I know the comics business. Harry Spiegel and Moe Shulman are prime suspects, and for the good of the Starr Syndicate, and perhaps for Americana Comics, too, we need them cleared."

His dark eyes had all the expression of the buttons on his coat. "If they're innocent."

"And brought to justice, fast, if they're guilty. Can you imagine how this could play in the papers?"

He grunted. "I've already pulled strings for this to be downplayed in the press, and Captain Chandler has agreed to be discreet about his investigation."

"How long can that last? Comic books are already getting a black eye, Louie—they're the primary cause of juvenile delinquency in our great country, or haven't you heard?"

"I've heard."

"This is the kind of bad public relations that could kill a healthy industry, and comic books are looking a little sick around the gills to me. And I don't just mean the Blue Barracuda."

He closed his eyes. Then he opened them and almost smiled. Almost. "All right. Let's say I agree with you. How can I be of help?"

I sat forward. "I have no shortage of suspects, Louie. But can you think of anything in recent days that would lead you to think I should look hard at one party or another?"

The damn sneer again. "I don't have any intention of playing the game of character assassination with my editorial staff."

"You need to stick a 'but' on the end of that, Louie, and tell me about Sy Mortimer."

"Tell you what?"

"I just spoke to him, Louie. He admits Donny was furious with him over this *Wonder Boy* catastrophe."

His hands were still folded over his belly, and his expression grew thoughtful. "Well . . . frankly, Donny asked me to fire Sy last week, but I ignored him. I figured it would blow over."

I leaned in. "If Sy's screwup costs you the *Wonder Guy* property, too, I'd think you'd want to fire the SOB yourself."

His expression looked pained, about a hangnail's worth. "It was more than just . . . frankly, Donny was irritated with Sy in general."

"Really? Why?"

"Sy has developed a proprietary interest in *Wonder Guy*. He's writing material himself, hiring his friends in the science-fiction field, and rewriting everybody's scripts . . . including Harry Spiegel's . . . to an insane degree."

"Sy seems to think he's improving *Wonder Guy*—thinks Spiegel is out of date."

His chin came up. "Short of all this maniacal rewriting, I happen to agree with him. I happen to agree with the steps he's taken to improve the property, and his efforts to minimize Spiegel and Shulman's out-of-touch approach. But Donny didn't."

"Why? Defending the creators? Just a different opinion . . . ?"

"None of that. Sy has begun taking credit for *Wonder Guy*. He's given interviews to magazines calling himself the driving force behind the feature. 'The Guy Behind *Wonder Guy*'—that was in *Collier's* last month. And that kind of thing trod on Donny's territory."

"His ego, you mean."

He actually smiled, though the mustache didn't notice. "Donny's ego took up . . . considerable territory."

I leaned an elbow on the table. "Louie, you say you agree with Sy's modernizing *Wonder Guy*?"

"I do."

"What about the creators of *Wonder Guy*? Where does that leave them?"

Now he worked up his best kindly look; you can guess how successful that was. "Jack, you know how fair we've been to the boys—hell, generous. But *we're* the businessmen."

"And they're the hired help?"

"Yes. Without publication, *Wonder Guy* would just be a bunch of drawings in a drawer back in Iowa. We pay them well— you and Maggie pay them well. I don't mean to diminish their role—back in the rag trade, we needed skilled cutters, didn't we? But cutters didn't control that business, and writers and artists don't control this one."

"I see."

He frowned and, oddly, the mustache twitched though his mouth wasn't doing a damn thing. "Do you? *We* spent the money on *Wonder Guy*, Jack. *We* took the risk. *We* made those two— they would be nothing without us, and where is their goddamned loyalty? If *Wonder Guy* had been a flop, who would've lost out? Not those ungrateful whelps. No, Donny and me."

"You and Donny." I smiled wistfully. "A great team. Still a team, Louie? Same in '48 as '38?"

He was pasty to begin with, but I'm sure he paled. "We are . . . were . . . still partners."

I shrugged. "I was just wondering if Donny had gone out of style, like Spiegel and Shulman. Donny wasn't like you, Louie— you're respectable. You give generous contributions to charity—you put a wing on that hospital out on Long Island, didn't you? You're not that same callow bookkeeper for girlie magazines, anymore, are you? The one who kept two sets of ledgers—one for you and Donny, one for Uncle Sam?"

And now a shade of red came up from his neck. "Keep that kind of foul thinking to yourself."

I gestured with an open hand. "You're a forward-looking businessman, Louie. Yours is the kind of professional face Americana needs."

"I don't have to put up with your crude sarcasm."

"You understand that you're in the business of children's entertainment—weren't you the one who gave the edict that *Wonder Guy* and *Batwing* and all of your characters were forbidden from killing bad guys? That was unacceptable behavior for an Americana superhero."

He stiffened and at long last the hands unfolded and disappeared beneath the table. "What's wrong with developing an acceptable code of behavior for our characters? Why not set a standard of civilized, responsible behavior that the young people of America can embrace?"

That sounded like it came from a speech he'd given at some comics publishers banquet.

"Why not? But what about *Donny's* behavior? He has a wife and a mistress, and how many of those Varga girls working for you has he compromised?"

Beet red. "This is outrageous . . . . You're going to have to leave, Jack."

"There've been rumors for years, Louie, that Donny wanted to leave Selma for Honey Daily—and that you talked him out of it. That's all you needed, a pissed-off ex-Mrs. Harrison as a stockholder. I noticed at the party you were pretty chummy with Selma."

He scooted back the chair and stood. Stiffly. "Jack . . . out of respect to the major—"

"The major would've been out of style, too, where you're concerned, with all his showgirls. You always kept at least a step removed from the likes of Frank Calabria, but Donny relished his mob ties. Big mistake. We're in the glorious postwar world, Louie, and you have to keep Americana respectable."

He leaned forward, put both hands on the table and finally showed real emotion—rage. "You're goddamned right I do! Do you know how I spent this morning, when I wasn't talking to idiot detectives about this ridiculous thing? I was on the phone with an advertiser willing to fund thirty-nine episodes of a *Wonder Guy* television show. Television, Jack! The future."

"A future with no place in it for a glad-handing, womanizing, drunken hale-fellow-well-met like Donny Harrison?"

He stood straight again, chin up. "I have nothing more to say to you, Jack."

I got up. "Yeah. Well, I understand. You're grieving."

Funny thing—when I glanced in at the secretarial pool on my way out, none of them seemed that sad, either.

When I'd called from the Waldorf this morning, Maggie had requested I join her and *Batwing* cartoonist Rod Krane for a business supper at the Strip Joint. She'd set it for 7 P.M., to give me plenty of time to go to the Harrison funeral and deal with whatever that entailed.

And it hadn't entailed much—a fairly quick cab ride to the Upper West Side, and back again.

The Harrisons may have lived in Long Island now, but Donny's funeral was a Manhattan affair, at the Riverside Memorial Chapel at Amsterdam Avenue and West Seventy-second; and Queens got in the mix when he was buried at Union Field Cemetery. The graveside services and the field trip it would have required I skipped; but the funeral played to a packed house of maybe 250.

No, Donny wasn't buried in his Wonder Guy outfit. Though he'd been about as religious as a tree stump, his wife or somebody had decided to deck Donny out in a purple-striped prayer shawl and a white skullcap, burying him as an Orthodox Jew. The casket was bronze-trimmed mahogany and probably cost about the same as a new Lincoln.

I picked out Louis Cohn and Sy Mortimer and even Rod Krane among the yarmulkes, though Rod was the only cartoonist I spotted. No surprise that Spiegel and Shulman had taken a pass, and obviously Honey Daily hadn't been invited. Donny's big chauffeur, Hank Morella—in a black suit, not his livery—sat next to the two Harrison kids, a boy and girl high-school age or thereabouts, Hank next to the boy (who gave Kaddish), Selma next to the girl. For a gentile employee, Hank rated pretty high, considering there was no shortage of Harrison relatives, not to mention Louie Cohn.

I made myself seen, but managed not to talk to anybody much and, feeling like I'd been sprung from stir, cabbed it back to the Starr Building, where I arrived just after four. The uniformed operator—a bright-eyed, depressingly cheerful eternal kid of forty-five called Pete, who played the horses, consistently lost and would probably kill himself someday with a big smile on his puss—took me up to the third floor. The small pale-walled dark-carpeted landing was home to only two doors, one a fire exit, the other to my apartment.

My three rooms, laid out in boxcar fashion, like the office floor and Maggie's digs, had been called cold and sterile by some. Those people didn't get asked back. The windowless living room was off-white walls with Bauhaus furniture, beautifully boxy black leather well-padded stuff with tubular trim and legs, a sofa facing my television set (the midcentury fireplace of American apartments), looking across a glass coffee table on a white area rug on the waxed wood floor with a chair on either side. To be sociable, I keep a well-stocked liquor cart.

The black-and-white motif was echoed by a handful of framed original comic strips, Sunday pages mostly (in their natural black-and-white uncolored state), gifts signed to the major or me over the years by our artists, as well as some of the competitors. Lots of these originals just got tossed or burned, but both the major and Maggie had respect for the work and returned it to the artists.

And the major's point of view had been that the stuff was better than anything the Picasso crowd was turning out, and if I didn't wholly agree, I sure couldn't afford anything by Pablo, so these fun free samples made do. Since the Bauhaus stuff gave the joint a modern look, I went for the more geometric comic strips, Chester Gould's *Dick Tracy* and George Herriman's *Krazy Kat* and Cliff Sterrett's *Polly and Her Pals* and, by way of loyalty to Starr Syndicate, Rod Krane's *Batwing*.

For a bachelor pad (as *Esquire* had recently taken to calling modern apartments for unmarried males), decorating the walls with what the unsophisticated female might consider "kid stuff" was a calculated risk. But it weeded out the humorless candidates, and even the most beautiful, stacked dish had better have a sense of funny if she's planning to hang around me for any length of time.

The comic-strip gallery also provided an appropriate backdrop when I would invite guests up here for a business talk, which Maggie appreciated, since we could entertain our writers and artists and editors and salesmen and subscribers easier up here than in the office, and more intimately than down in the Strip Joint.

The bedroom was the next link in the chain, the windowless walls a warm yellow and the modern approach continued by blond Heywood-Wakefield furnishings, double bed with rust-color satin spread and twin nightstands, highboy chest with a mirror over it, and a neatly arranged desk, since I didn't keep an office elsewhere. The desktop was almost always clear, stuff put away when I was done to leave a nice clean surface—clutter kills the modernist look. The only exception was a framed photo of the major and my mother in a sleek silver frame dating to the '20s.

No comic art in here, but a couple of passable ersatz Pablos were spotted around, thanks to a Village art show where I'd splurged fifty bucks on three paintings. One nightstand had a panther lamp with square Chinese shade, dark green; the other a white phone. I usually keep the paperback I'm reading on it—right now, *I, the Jury*.

The bathroom was off the bedroom, to the right, small but modern and white with a walk-in shower. During the war, Maggie had thoughtfully remodeled this floor—which had been used for storage by the previous tenants—into living space for her stepson, and it awaited me when I returned from service, a nice surprise. And, in truth, a smart move on her part, because without it (and its rent-free status), I might have turned down the vice presidency.

As for the kitchen, it was modern and white and way too big for my needs, but I did sit at the white-speckled black Formica table from time to time, as I dined on Coca-Cola and deli cold cuts and maybe rye bread, which was about the extent of my mastery of the culinary arts. On the Sunday nights I was in town, the table served up poker and chips (red, blue, white and potato) to some buddies of mine in the newspaper and show business games.

So that's the layout, and on this particular afternoon the pad was spotless as a furniture showroom, if considerably more eccentric, a combo of my own neatness yen—military school had drilled it in me, and the real army hadn't exactly cured me—and the twice-a-week cleaning lady.

The only thing that still needed cleaning was me—I admit I'd gone to Donny's funeral without stopping back to shower, and by late afternoon of a July day, even an overcast one, I was getting ripe. I must have stayed in under the hot needles for twenty minutes, just letting them pound on me, maybe hoping to get some sense drummed in.

Soon I was on my couch, in my boxers and T-shirt and socks, with a bottle of Coke in one hand and today's *Daily News* in the other. The coverage of Donny's death continued to call it an accidental death, albeit "as wild as anything the funny pages could conjure." Seemed to me that the funny pages didn't conjure a damn thing—that was the job of writers and cartoonists—but I was starting to wonder if Captain Chandler was a conjurer, keeping the murder aspect hush-hush.

Of course, like Scarlett O'Hara said, tomorrow was another day; and murders don't stay mum in Manhattan, not with a cast of characters like this one, they didn't.

I was tired. Partly I was tired because I'd only had a quick bite for lunch at Lindy's—half a pastrami and Swiss—before my excursion to the west side to pay Donny my halfhearted respects, and after I'd walked over to a building on Forty-third where at the Hirsch chemical laboratory I dropped off the carpet-thread samples from the Donny-sized stain on his mistress's apartment floor.

But also I was worn out from talking to suspects like Frank Calabria, Sy Mortimer and Louis Cohn, not to mention Hank Morella and Honey Daily herself. I'm sure you're impressed by how incisive my queries were and how snappy my comebacks; but what you can't know is how goddamned exhausting it was.

Cops aren't born with flat feet, you know, neither do they come out of the womb with those hangdog, world-weary, cynical expressions. Or so I've been told.

Anyway, I fell asleep on the sofa and the phone called me to the bedroom for an answer and a bartender's voice I recognized, from the Strip Joint below, said, "Jack, Maggie's waiting. And some sharpie."

"What time is it?"

"Quarter after seven."

"Shit," I said.

"You're welcome," he said.

"Tell her five minutes."

"They're in her private room."

I thanked the bartender, whose name was Ed, and hung up and threw on a lightweight short-sleeve white shirt, slung on a dark gray silk necktie, and climbed into a lightweight flannel suit, lighter gray, then stepped into my moccasin-style loafers. Since I was just headed downstairs, I skipped the hat.

The fire exit stairs were the only way to access the restaurant from inside the building, and I took those, and went down the little side corridor off the stairs that emptied out toward the rear of the restaurant, into an area of restrooms in the space between the dining room and the kitchen.

Maggie's small private dining room was tucked back in that same general region, and I opened the door and entered the compact if not quite cramped space whose four white walls each had a different large formal black-and-white photograph of Maggie, glamour head shots but no stripper trappings. The round linen-covered table (with red roses, stem-clipped, floating in a glass bowl as a centerpiece) would accommodate six comfortably and eight when it had to, but normally had four chairs, and right now two were filled by Maggie Starr and Rod Krane.

Maggie wore a form-fitting short-sleeved black dress with a narrow but deep neckline, a double strand of pearls dipping down into her hint of cleavage; her makeup was light but her bee-stung lips were a confident bright red. Her red hair was in a loose-curled do that likely meant a hairdresser pal of Bryce's had made a house call. She was not quite in full battle array but was obviously a few pounds shy of coming out of her self-imposed exile.

I knew how she would describe herself, in this state: "Almost human." Most women would kill to look half that human.

Krane wore a white dinner jacket and a black bow tie, stupidly overdressed for the occasion. Blade-thin, well tanned, with a long narrow nose no plastic surgeon had anything to do with, and gleaming white teeth, he was a handsome devil, but too aware of it, always smirking to work his dimples and winking to engage the slashes of dark eyebrow, the black widow's-peaked hair slicked back like George Raft fifteen years ago.

Maggie's drink, in a collins glass, was a Horse's Neck—ginger ale and whiskey, with a spiral of lemon peel and a few ice cubes. That was all she drank—years ago somebody at a party had handed her one, saying, "A peel for a peeler," and she hated the remark but loved the drink.

Krane was having a martini, probably thinking it went well with his man-about-town attire. At least tonight he was sparing us his cigarette-holder routine.

I had a hunch Krane was on at least his second martini, because he had a loose-limbed manner, waving and smiling too wide upon seeing me. Maggie, I would wager, was on her first Horse's Neck. She was smiling just a little and her sideways look at her guest indicated her and my purposes would best be served by lubricating him thoroughly.

"We already ordered," Maggie said, smiling at me but with half-lidded eyes that further endorsed Krane's pickled condition. "We're having the strip steak."

"Fine," I said, sitting next to Maggie and across from Krane. We all had plenty of arm room at the big round table.

"Best strip steak in town," Krane said, "for the best strip artist in America, courtesy of the best stripteaser in the world."

"Why thank you, Rod," she said, voice warm, eyes icy, "you're much too kind."

A barmaid, in white shirt, black tie and tuxedo pants, entered with a tray bearing a fresh martini for Krane and my first Coke on ice. She was a blonde pushing thirty (gently), one of the numerous between-gigs dancers who worked the Strip Joint.

After she replaced his empty cocktail glass with a filled one, he leered up at her and said, "Nicely done!"

She wasn't good enough an actress for her smile and "Thank you" to play, but Krane didn't seem to notice, witty bon vivant that he was.

He sipped his martini and said to me, "Saw you at the service this afternoon, Jackie."

Nobody calls me Jackie. I despise being called Jackie.

"Yeah. Quite a crowd."

"You know what they say—give the people what they want, and they'll turn out."

I actually smiled at that—like they say, even a stopped clock is right twice a day—but Maggie said, "You shouldn't be disrespectful, Rod. Donny was a big part of your life. Gave you your big break."

"Come on, Maggie," he said with a leer, teeth startlingly white in that tan face. "Don't kid a kidder."

He didn't notice her tiny, tiny wince; but I did.

Krane sipped his martini and continued: "I mean, *you* didn't bother to show. You sent your lackey Jackie here in your place."

I decided not to hit him for that; would have spoiled the mood.

As for Maggie, she shrugged a little; her faint smile would have appeared amused to anybody but me, who read it as contemptuous. "Somebody had to run the syndicate."

"Come on, Mag—you didn't like Donny any better than I did, than *any* of us did."

Another modest shrug. "Actually, I didn't know Donny all that well. The major was close to him. And Jack knew him, growing up. But I've done most of my business dealings with Louie Cohn."

He pointed a gun-like finger at her and winked. "Smart girl. Proof positive that just 'cause a doll has a fine frame on her doesn't mean she don't have what it takes, upstairs, in the brains department."

God, I hated this guy. Donny was no great shakes as a human being, but talk about worthy murder victims . . . .

Maggie was saying, "You prefer dealing with Louie, then?"

His narrow eyes widened. "God, yes! Donny had a wild streak, and he could cop an attitude and just not let it *go*—if he decided you were trying to screw him over, there was no room for negotiation. No room for reasonable discourse."

"Whereas," Maggie said, "Louie is more conservative. Takes a longer, wiser view."

"Bingo."

Salads came, crisp lettuce with chopped carrot and celery and a tangy vinegar and oil Italian, the house dressing.

As we ate, Krane bragged about Hollywood interest in a second *Batwing* serial, and mentioned half a dozen pending licensing deals for toys, Halloween costumes and candy tie-ins. For all his bluster, and for as well as the *Batwing* book sold, Krane and his feature had never managed the licensing muscle of Spiegel and Shulman's creation. No radio show, for example, and the TV series talk was strictly *Wonder Guy*.

When the steaks came, all medium rare with baked potato on

a side plate, the talk continued, Krane doing most of it. This was aided by a fourth martini arriving midway through the meal. I mostly ate, being fairly starved and not wanting to waste jaw action on talk. And I was pleased to see Maggie eating more than just a salad, though her potato was jaybird naked of butter or sour cream, and she ate only a third or so of the meat, which was at least as criminal as the murder of Donny Harrison.

Krane's bragging had to do with his, and our, knowledge that his five-year contract with Starr for the *Batwing* comic strip would come up next year. We were also aware that his ten-year contract with Americana would be due for renewal next year, as well—about six months after Spiegel and Shulman's. Krane knew the comic-strip version of *Batwing* was doing only fair and wanted to keep us impressed with the property—make us perceive it as a going, growing concern and not a fad whose moment had passed.

"There's a rumor," Maggie said, "that you and the *Wonder* boys are throwing in together, to hit Americana up for a negotiation simultaneously. Form a united front."

This was news to me; but Maggie had her ways.

"It's been discussed," Krane said, pushing his plate away. He'd close to cleaned it, leaving nothing but a shred of baked potato skin as evidence of the meal. He was one of those live-wire skinny guys who could eat a horse and still weigh in like a jockey.

"Strength in numbers," Maggie said.

"Yeah." Krane flipped a hand. "And I've been thinking of going that route. Some pretty nice leverage, there. Americana would hardly like to lose its two biggest properties at once."

I asked, "How could Americana lose rights they already own?"

Krane's grin was like a joker's in a deck of cards. "We could challenge those rights. The boys have a case to make, thanks to Sy Mortimer's foul-up with *Wonder Boy*. And I have a trick up my *Batwing* as well."

Maggie smiled warmly at him, but I saw the ice crystalize in her eyes; she made herself reach out and touch Krane's sleeve. "What trick is that, Rod? We're all friends here."

"Right. Aren't you an Americana shareholder?"

"Just a few shares the major left me. My biggest concern is that the Starr Syndicate is still able to syndicate *Batwing* and *Wonder Guy*."

I noticed she gave Krane top billing, which he didn't deserve. Maggie knew what she was doing.

She was saying, "If that means Starr dealing with Americana, so be it; but if *you* wind up with the rights to *Batwing*, well . . . it would only simplify the syndication contract."

This was BS of a rarefied order, and I don't know if Krane would have bought it, had not his fourth martini been deader than Donny.

"I have no intention of leaving Americana," Krane said, "as long as they treat me with the respect I deserve."

Anything short of pushing him down an elevator shaft would qualify by that standard.

"And the trick up your wing," Maggie said, and smiled wickedly, and sipped her Horse's Neck, "makes that possible? Come on, Rod—spill."

The joker's grin again. "Okay. Good thing you're sitting

down . . . . My entire contract with Americana is invalid. According to my old man."

Hiram Cohen (Krane's father) was an attorney who represented many garment factories, including one of the city's largest, which happened to be run by Hiram's brother.

"I hope *our* contract isn't invalid," Maggie said lightly.

"Probably not. You see, I wasn't of legal age when I signed with Donny—only twenty. That means, anytime I care to walk into Louis Cohn's office, it's a whole new ball game for *Batwing*."

Meaning a major-league jam for Americana—*both* its top properties facing possible reversion to the creators, in Spiegel and Shulman's case thanks to the *Wonder Boy* fubar, and in Krane's a contract voided because the cartoonist had been a minor at signing.

"You have the birth certificate to prove it?" Maggie asked.

"No. My father was an immigrant, and you know how these old Jews were about such documents—papers like that tended to get lost in the shuffle. But my father and mother will testify that I was born in 1915."

No records to subpoena, then.

I said, "But your father negotiated the first contract—did he build this in on purpose?"

"Don't be insulting," Krane said, but he was grinning again. "My father was a simple immigrant. His math skills were deficient."

Krane's "simple immigrant" father had studied law books at home and taken (and passed) the bar, becoming the top garment-center attorney in town.

Maggie asked, "Had you told Donny Harrison about your invalid contract yet?"

"Hell no, Mag! My father and I were in full agreement about that."

I asked, "About what?"

"About going to *Louie Cohn* with this," Krane said, "and not Donny. God knows how that hotheaded son of a bitch Harrison would've reacted. Louie, now *he's* a businessman."

Maggie flicked a look at me just as I was flicking one her way: the well-lubricated Krane had just traded us one murder motive for four martinis.

And maybe Krane *had* told Donny about this minor ploy, and gotten such a bad reaction that removing the publisher, to make way for the more "reasonable" Louie Cohn, had been a tempting option.

The blonde barmaid brought me a second Coke, Krane a fifth martini, while Maggie continued to nurse her first and only Horse's Neck.

Maggie asked, in a manner so casual it could hardly have been more calculated, "What's this I hear about Will Hander and Donny?"

No grin. In fact Krane frowned and his deep dimples went AWOL, though the laugh crinkles around the dark eyes tightened and his forehead creased over the black brush strokes of eyebrow. "What *about* Will?"

Will Hander was widely believed to have been the co-creator of *Batwing*, but had got none of the credit and only freelancer money for the writing.

"I've heard," Maggie said, "that for several years he's been pressuring Donny to give him his rightful share of the strip."

"What *he* considers his 'rightful share'!" Krane snapped. "Listen, Maggie, we've talked about this before. *Batwing* was mine—my concept, my character. Will was just the writer I went to, to flesh out my script notions."

"I don't mean to step on any toes," Maggie said with a smile so charming I damn near checked my back pocket for my wallet, "but scuttlebutt has it that Will created Sparrow, and lots of the villains, including Harlequin and Tuxedo."

Sparrow was Batwing's kid sidekick.

Krane's nostrils flared, and his eyes slitted. "Believing scuttlebutt is beneath you, Maggie. I'm like any other major cartoonist, except that because I have both comic strips *and* comic books to provide material for, I need more help than most. I value Will—he's the best *Batwing* writer. I'm second to nobody in my admiration for his work. But he's just a writer."

Right—the way the half dozen *Batwing* cartoonists salted here and there around the New York environs were just artists. Where big-time comics creators like Milton Caniff or Sam Fizer or Hal Rapp openly admitted having studios wherein they worked with their assistants—even posing for group pictures and making their staff's names public—Krane kept his anonymous "helpers" out of touch with each other, and scattered.

Even the laziest, least talented cartoonists usually did *some* work on their own strips—doing rough layouts, say, or inking the faces. But I suspected the last pen Krane touched was to write a check, and his last brush had been stuck in his mouth, working to make those teeth so goddamn white.

"I guess what I'm getting to," Maggie said, "is whether you think Will might've had a motive for killing Donny."

"Oh."

Krane's face relaxed, now that the subject had gone from something serious—whether he was a money and credit hog—to something trivial—like his chief writer having killed their publisher.

"Well," he said, "sure. Maybe. Donny paid Will directly, you know, at my request . . . and paid him well. I don't think Donny would've took kindly to being squeezed like that."

Or taken kindly to Krane's lawyer poppa putting the squeeze on him, either.

Krane hadn't touched the fifth martini yet. Maybe the gin was catching up to him. He looked at Maggie, carefully, doing his best to bring her in focus; then he looked at me the same way. He was weaving just a little.

Finally he said, "What's this about, fellas and girls? I thought this was a business supper. See how *Batwing*'s doing. Kind of lay the groundwork for our new contract. And I wasn't a minor when I signed with Starr, so you should have nothin' to worry about there."

"Good," Maggie said.

"You're asking me about . . . you're talking about . . . this is about . . . the *murder*. Right? Donny's murder?"

"Yes," she said.

And I nodded.

"Well," he said. "*Why?* That's . . . police business. I already talked to that Captain Chandler. He seemed like the genuine article. He'll get to the bottom of it, right?"

Maggie said, "Eventually."

I said, "I'm checking into the circumstances, Rod. To protect our interests. Some of our most valued talents are on the suspect list."

"Oh. Sure. Like Harry and Moe?"

"Yes . . . among others."

He frowned. "Well, hell, *I'm* not a suspect."

I grinned. "Good to hear. But maybe you can help me out with zeroing in on some real suspects."

"Yeah. Sure. Why not? Shoot."

I leaned back, folded my arms. "Let's start with Honey Daily."

He smirked, shook his head. "She can't be a suspect. She was Donny's girl."

"But she was also *your* girl, wasn't she? For a while, anyway?"

I don't know if I ever saw anybody sober up quicker.

Krane said, "Uh . . . who says?"

"She does. She also says you can't take no for an answer."

His jaw had dropped. "What's that supposed to mean?"

"That when Miss Daily gave you your walking papers, you didn't take the hint. And threatened to go to Donny about it."

He was squirming; kind of fun to see a guy in a white dinner jacket squirm. "Well . . . come on, Jackie. You know how it is when a love affair goes on the rocks."

"No. Tell me how it is. And the name is 'Jack.'"

The flickering smile was nervous, as were the darting eyes. "I . . . I was crazy about her. When she said it was over, I said all kinds of stupid, lunatic things. Raving and ranting things. . . . You don't *really* think I'd tell Donny about Honey and me?"

"She said you told her you were going to 'stick it to Donny,' "
I said. "You knew about his diabetes, right? Or am I just adding
insulin to injury?"

The black eyebrows rose so high, they damn near straightened
out into exclamation points. "Jack! Please! Of course I knew
about his diabetes, everybody knew about Donny's diabetes, and
his shots and . . . I just *told* you how I was gonna 'stick it' to
Donny! By my pop sticking it to *Americana*, with the bit about
me being a minor when I signed *Batwing* over!"

Now it was a "bit."

Maggie said, "Do you think you were the first, Rod?"

"The first . . . what?"

"The first man Honey Daily strayed with, away from Donny?"

"Hell no! Donny was just her meal ticket—she only saw him a
couple days a week, or I should say nights. I was just one of many.
One of a parade of chumps who rolled through that suite, helping
keep her mind off the monster she had to pay the rent to."

I asked, "Who else was on that list?"

Besides me, currently.

The joker grin returned. "I don't know 'em all. Maybe she
keeps a little black book, like horny bachelors do."

I gave him something that was half grin, half sneer. "Why, do
you have one?"

He stood and the martini glass spilled and sopped the linen. He
leaned his hands on the table, finding dry places, and said, "I'm
not the only Americana number in that little black book, that
much I'll tell you."

Maggie's voice had an edge. "Who, Rod? Who else from Americana?"

"Why should I tell you?" he said to her imperiously. Then to me, he snarled, "You're the one playing private eye—it's somebody *powerful*, that much I'll tell you. Maybe the most powerful man at Americana! Figure it out for yourself."

He left the table, paused at the door and said, "Thanks for the steak, and the martinis—now I know how a dame feels when you ply her with liquor to take advantage."

"Will it change your style?" I asked cheerfully, and he was gone.

"Hope he isn't driving," Maggie said, with a roll of her big green eyes.

"If he is," I said, "let's hope he kills nobody but himself, or maybe his ego."

"That would take a big crash."

I sat forward. "Have you been doing some sleuthing yourself, Maggie?"

Her smile was genuinely amused now. "Why? Some of my questions surprise you?"

"Yeah. I hate it when you know more than me."

"Life must be very uncomfortable for you, then." She had another sip of Horse's Neck. "Did you drop those thread samples off at that lab, as I suggested?"

"Yes. That stain can't be blood."

"Donny was sweating profusely, you said."

"Right."

She shrugged a little. "Maybe it was dye residue from the Wonder Guy costume, released by Donny's perspiration."

"Maybe. We'll know tomorrow. You think Rod is our killer?"

She sighed, making me uncomfortable—not because she knew more than me, but because she was my stepmother and when her breasts made themselves known under a garment like that, I squirmed.

"Rod our killer?" she mused. "Could we be so lucky?"

Once again I dropped by Honey Daily's suite at the Waldorf without calling. Whether I was hoping (or hoping not) to find her with another man—maybe someone powerful from Americana like Sy Mortimer or even Louis Cohn—I can't say. I do know knocking unannounced on any woman's door at nine at night is unspeakably rude. But I did it anyway.

I passed the peephole test and the door opened, with her in the same black dressing gown with its touches of pink, some of it ribbon, some of it her. Her hair was a lovely blonde tangle tickling her shoulders and the only makeup she had on was a little lipstick.

She leaned a red-nailed hand against the jamb and gave me a smile I didn't deserve. "You think you can just show up and get away with it, do you?"

"Worked before," I said. My hat, a light gray Milan that went well with my suit, was in hands. "I'm an impulsive boy."

"No phone at your place?"

I shrugged. "Suppose you'd said no?"

"Jack, Jack, Jack . . . you have more confidence than that, surely. . . . Come on in."

I followed her and her Chanel No. 5 through the foyer into the coral-and-emerald living room. She wasn't drinking anything. A radio was playing Cugat and his Latin stylings, and I quickly gathered it was a broadcast from this very hotel's Starlight Roof. A copy of the paperback of *Forever Amber* was open to her place on the coffee table by the sofa. The painting of the courtesan on the cover was almost as beautiful as Honey.

She sat and I sat. Next to her. Very next to her. She turned her face to mine and I kissed her. She kissed back. We kissed a while. Let's face it, kissing went on. Lots of it. And some fondling. We were of age.

Then she said, "You're troubled."

"No, I feel fine. Anyway, better."

The big baby blues showed genuine concern; or really well-done fake genuine concern. "You want to talk about it? It's the murder case, right? You've been looking into it all day?"

"All day except for when I was at the funeral."

She swallowed; turned away, looking toward the unlit fire place. Folded her arms. Sore point?

"Would you have liked to've gone?" I asked.

She said nothing.

"I'm not sure I know how you felt about him."

She shook her head. "I told you. I was fond of him. Very fond of him. He was good to me. I loved him, in my way. And everybody got to say good-bye to him but me."

I didn't point out that, on the list of people who got to say good-bye to Donny, the guy's wife and kids came first, along with their feelings about who they shared Donny's public farewell with. But, hell, she knew that. She was either feeling sorry for herself, or putting on a show for me.

And it bothered me, in fact pissed me off, that I couldn't tell the difference.

"Listen, Honey," I said, in a way that made the "H" ambiguous as to whether it was her name or an endearment, "you've been open to helping me. Giving me information, and sharing your opinions . . . so I can find Donny's killer."

"Yes. Yes, of course. I'll tell you anything you want to know."

"I'm glad to hear that." I slipped an arm around her shoulder. "Guess who I had the pleasure of dining with this evening?"

"I was kind of hoping it would be me," she said, and pouted, or pretended to. "But you didn't call."

"No, I had a prior engagement. Maggie Starr lined it up and played hostess—I ate with the talented and charming creator of *Batwing*."

She shuddered. "That creep Krane?"

"That creep Krane. And he told us his side of your affair."

"*His* side?" Her eyes flared. Nostrils, too. It was pretty, and pretty disturbing. "You make that sound like *my* side was . . . was what? Untrustworthy? A lie?"

"Honey—I'm investigating. I hear everybody's side, and I take into consideration which end of the telescope each person is looking through. Not talking lies or untrustworthiness, here. Just looking at the various perspectives."

"You're treading water, Jack."

And I was.

I cut straight to the point. "Baby, this son of a bitch says he was only one of a . . . he implied a large group."

"Group of what?"

Again I was blowing it.

I tried another angle. "You said it yourself—you had a life, aside from, away from, Donny. There were other men in your life. Like Rod, for a while."

Her eyes no longer flared; they tightened, so much so I could barely tell how she could see out of them. "I never denied it. I don't deny it. I was with Donny for a long, long time. And I am a normal woman with normal needs."

"Sure. I know. But what *I* need is to know . . . who were those other men?"

"*What?*"

"Honey—baby. I'm looking into the murder of the guy who paid for this suite. I need you to share the names of the other men who've, well, been in your life."

She drew away. "Don't 'honey baby' me, Jack Starr. This is out of line. *You* are out of line."

My arm no longer around her, I patted the air with peaceful palms. "Okay. Let's just limit it to Americana. Krane says you were seeing another bigwig at Americana, besides Donny."

"What? He's *lying*! That's *crazy*!"

"Nobody at all in your life, who had anything to do with Americana—Louie Cohn, maybe?"

Her face turned white. "Louie Cohn? My idea of having someone besides Donny Harrison in my life would have been to entertain *Louie Cohn*? *That* bloodless bastard?"

I knew it was a dumb thing to say. Cohn really was a bloodless bastard. You can't have an erection without having blood to send in that general direction.

She sat with her arms folded and the white in her face was going away and red coming in. Very tightly she said, "Jack, right now there is only one man in my life. Or at least there *was*—you. If you want to pursue that role, you need to get off this subject."

"Honey, it's not jealousy, or prying. I need the information to—"

Without looking at me, she said, "Jack, I need you to leave. I need you to leave right now."

Actually, that was fine with me.

But I said, "I hope we can get past this. I really do care about you, Honey."

"I care about you, too. But, Jack?"

"Yes?"

"Next time—call."

They called Jackson Heights the cornfields of Queens, because this middle-class community of single homes and garden apartments had been carved out of farmland. North of Roosevelt Avenue, centering around Eighty-second Street, the Heights was an active, well-off (if not quite well-to-do) Jewish enclave. On one of its greenest streets, in a colonial-style apartment building, Harry Spiegel lived with his young bride, Rose.

Their place, on the top floor, was spacious with the sort of nice, new furnishings a young couple starting out might assemble, assuming they had a little *mazuma*. The rose-color walls had ivory-framed pastel airbrushed floral prints that seemed an unlikely backdrop for a frenetic guy like Harry, who had whipped up the world's first comic-book superhero out of his adolescent imagination. Feeling like I'd walked into a *Better Homes & Gardens* layout, I was seated on a wine-color mohair sofa next to

Harry, and in a nearby matching lounge chair was Harry and Moe's attorney, Bert Zelman.

This was the morning after Honey Daily turned me away from her Waldorf suite. First thing, after breakfast at Walgreen's off Times Square, I had set up several meetings today—two in Queens and another out on Long Island, which meant I'd had a good excuse to play with my newest toy, my military-green '48 Ford Super Deluxe convertible, which I kept in a garage on Forty-fourth.

And the day was beautiful and sunny and pleasantly warm, perfect to glide along with the top down (my fedora on the rider's side floor) and go out to see how the other half lived. I was wearing a sky-blue shortsleeve shirt with striped tie under the cream-color linen jacket of my lightweight summer suit.

In the living room of the apartment, I met Rose Spiegel for the first time, but can't say I got to know her much. She was a small, pretty, dark-haired woman, just a little plump, in a yellow house-dress; she smiled and said hellos and got everybody glasses of iced tea with lemon and coasters for the end tables. And disappeared.

Yet her presence was all around me. The Sears catalogue decorating and the absence of any *Wonder Guy* trappings gave me the feeling she was not vitally involved in her husband's work.

Bright-eyed Harry was in a sportshirt—light yellow, with brown trousers—but the big, blocky lawyer wore a suit, a blue and white striped seersucker, with a blue-and-red bow tie on a pale blue shirt. About forty, Zelman had broad shoulders and, despite his sizeable gut, looked more square than round. The lawyer had the kind of jagged, expressive dark eyebrows cartoonists specialized in, a strong jaw worthy of Wonder Guy, and intense, intelligent brown eyes, with wavy brown hair swept back off a broad, expansive brow. A big man, he made Harry look like a kid on the couch next to me, or a midget.

"You understand I'm not a criminal lawyer," Zelman said, chewing on a big unlighted cigar (Rose had sweetly forbidden him to smoke), "but when Harry called me, and said you were coming over, I thought I should sit in. Hope you don't mind."

"More the merrier," I said, took a sip of iced tea (sweetened—ugh!) and returned the tall glass to its coaster. "My role in this is to help clear Harry and Moe."

The expression on his pie-pan mug painfully earnest, Harry said, "Listen, Jack, I don't mean to be ungrateful to you or Maggie, but I don't *need* clearing. I didn't *do* anything."

"I don't think you did." I said.

He gestured with both hands; he did that a lot. "So why not wait for the cops to just do their job?"

I glanced at Zelman, who smiled knowingly as he rolled the cigar around in thick lips.

"Harry," I said, "the cops move slow. The Homicide Bureau has probably ten more murders on their hands, since Donny belly flopped on that blade."

"Fifteen," Zelman said.

I went on: "Plus, the coppers have to dot every 'i' and cross every 't.' Add to that my inside knowledge of the business, and the players, and I may be able to do us all some good."

Zelman leaned out from his comfortable chair to put a supportive hand on his client's arm. "Harry, I think Mr. Starr is right. He can only help in this matter."

I said, "We have another day gone by without the press picking up on the murder aspect. Captain Chandler is keeping the lid on, God knows how."

Harry frowned. "Why is *that* a good thing?"

Brother. "Oh, I don't know, Harry—maybe you think it'd be *good* publicity, having *Wonder Guy* in the headlines next to a murder?"

The writer frowned in embarrassment. "Oh. I hadn't thought about it like that . . ."

"No," I said, and let the edge into my tone, "you're too relieved to have Donny Harrison out of the way to look at this in the cold, hard light it deserves."

His pupils were like exclamation marks in his wide eyes. "Jack! That's not fair!"

"Neither is life, except maybe on the funny pages." I braved another sip of the sweetened tea. "Harry, you and Moe are prime suspects here—not the *only* ones, but—"

Harry was shaking his head so hard, his hair was flapping. "Jack, Donny had more enemies than Hitler. Why look at *us*?"

"You've talked to Chandler? Or did he send some of his men around?"

Harry glanced at Zelman, who gave him nothing, just kept chewing that cigar. Finally the writer said, "It was Chandler, personally. He was nice enough. Had me sign a couple comic books to his kids. Would he ask me to do that if he suspected me?"

Zelman closed his eyes.

I said, "Did Chandler mention the theory they're pursuing, about how Donny died?"

"Yeah." Harry paused to have a sip of his own iced tea. "He said Donny was poisoned."

"Did he say what *kind* of poison?"

"No."

"Did he ask you whether you knew about Donny's diabetes? About the insulin Donny took regularly?"

Harry frowned in confusion. "Yeah. But he didn't say why."

"Did he ask you whether you knew Donny kept insulin bottles at various locations? Like at home, and at work, and his girl-friend's?"

"Yeah, he did." Harry shrugged. "And I said I did."

"Did he question you alone, or with Moe present?"

"Alone."

"Did he mention Moe's diabetes?"

"Uh, no."

"Did you mention it?"

"No."

I glanced at Zelman, who looked grave and a little ill. Then to Harry I said, "They think somebody spiked Donny's insulin. The fact that Moe has diabetes, and is familiar with the trappings, well . . ."

Zelman straightened and said, "You don't have to have dia-betes to know about sufferers giving themselves insulin shots."

"No," I admitted. "But it's just the kind of suggestive detail that starts cops thinking, and sways juries."

The lawyer couldn't argue against that point.

Harry's complexion was white and his expression grim. "Are you trying to *scare* me, Jack?"

"Yes."

"Why? What *good* does it do?"

I bled all of the smart-ass tone from my voice, which took some doing; I met the writer's eyes and held them. "First, if you did this—or if you know or believe that Moe did it—you need to say nothing more to me, and you need to have Mr. Zelman here get you a good criminal attorney."

"Jesus . . ."

"And, Harry, I'd advise you to tell that attorney to call Maggie or me, so I can back off on this investigation, and not bring you any more trouble than you already have."

He was shaking his head again, hair flopping. "Jack, I swear on my mother's grave that I did not do this thing. And I don't have any reason to believe Moe did, either—and, please, be *serious*. There's no gentler soul on the face of the earth than Moe Shulman!"

I glanced at Zelman, who smiled a little around that cigar. I allowed myself a smile, too.

"Okay," I said. "I believe you. And I'm going to stay at it. Actually, I've been at it ever since I got that call in the office, from the cops, while you and Moe were in to talk to Maggie about *Funny Guy*."

Harry brightened. "Have you decided? Do we have a deal?"

Zelman closed his eyes again.

I said, "Harry—do you really think the Starr Syndicate is going to sign a new contract with the prime suspects in a murder case? That's a big part of why I have to clear this thing up, and fast."

"Oh. Oh, God. I see."

This time I was the one who gestured with both hands. "We would love to keep doing business with you and Moe. But we aren't prepared to accept packages of comic strips from a studio based out of Sing Sing."

"I . . . I understand. This is terrible. Really terrible."

Finally Donny's death seemed something other than a boon to Harry Spiegel.

I addressed Zelman. "There's no shortage of suspects in this case, but I can tell you that the renegotiation of the *Wonder Guy* . . . and, for that matter, *Batwing* . . . contracts may well play a role."

Zelman said, "If so, let me assure you, Mr. Starr, that Harry and Moe had no reason to do away with Donny Harrison. If all I wanted to do was sue for back compensation—the licensing money that the boys have been diddled out of—a fortune could be made. But I have a way to get them the full rights back . . . putting us in the catbird seat, and Americana in, if you'll pardon my French, the shitter."

I nodded. "Mortimer's screwup with *Wonder Boy*, right?"

Zelman flinched just a little, not pleased that I knew about his secret weapon; but otherwise he only smiled. "Yes. That opened the door. Americana will soon be doing business on our terms."

"And Harrison wasn't a stumbling block?"

His smile was wide and a touch patronizing. "Hardly. It's Louis Cohn who's the negotiator."

One more sickening-sweet sip of iced tea; then, casually I said to the lawyer, "And I understand you plan to join forces with Rod Krane."

Again Zelman was clearly not pleased that I was ahead of his game. He removed the unlit cigar and gestured with it. "We are considering that. Krane's father is a shrewd if self-taught attorney, who has his own barrel to put Americana over."

I nodded. "The 'barrel' being that Krane was a minor when he signed the original contract. Do you *believe* that?"

Zelman's small self-satisfied smile was of a type that had in human history appeared on no face other than a lawyer's.

"No," he said. "But I also know there's no way for Americana to prove Krane wasn't underage. Their whole comic-book applecart could turn over on them, in an instant—where are they without their two top superheroes?"

F orest Hills, another popular Queens middle-class garden community, rested on the wooded heights at the northeast end of Forest Park. Colonial and English Tudor homes abounded, as did apartment houses, almost all with well-tended landscaped lawns that made a piker out of anything in Jackson Heights.

In a ten-room colonial, Moe Shulman lived with the family he'd brought out from Des Moines—parents, two brothers and a sister. In a large upstairs room, which must have started out in life as a master bedroom, Moe had fashioned a studio for himself and four assistants.

This was a smaller version of the bullpen of cartoonists at Americana, a suburban bedroom transposed into a blue-smoke-filled den of creativity, with considerably more mote-dappled sun-light coming in than you'd find on Lexington Avenue.

The cartoonists hunkered at their drawing boards—this one inking, this one penciling, this one lettering, another inking a cover—were men in their late twenties and early thirties, in sportshirts or short-sleeve white ones, sans tie. Three of the four assistants wore glasses, though none could compete with the bug-eye-inducing lenses of the man in charge, *Wonder Guy* co-creator Moe Shulman.

Moe and I sat on a couch against one wall as the men worked, rarely talking to one another, sunk deep in their artistic efforts. I had a bottle of Coke that Moe's mom had given me, before showing me to the stairs, and Moe was drinking hot black coffee, despite the warmth of the July day and the lack of air-conditioning (a window fan was doing a pretty decent job of stirring up a breeze).

Moe was in a short-sleeve white shirt. He'd been working at a drawing board, penciling rough layouts. This didn't surprise me— I doubted with his eyesight he could manage much more, these days.

He had taken time to introduce me around—two of the four guys had made the trek from Des Moines, childhood friends of the boys from their fanzine days; two others had names I recognized, because Maggie had done some snooping a while back to see which Shulman ghosts might come in handy for the syndicated strip version of *Wonder Guy*, should the boys ever get forced out by Americana. The latter was not a possibility we looked forward to, but reality is reality.

Now we were on the couch, an old springy thing, and Moe said, "I'm glad you came to see me."

"Oh?"

"Yeah. I mean . . . without Harry around."

"Why is that?"

His expression was at once sad and kind, the enlarged eyes behind the lenses wide but not childlike. He was a bigger man than his partner, with a full head of dark brown hair graying here and there.

He said, "Harry gets upset. There are things I can't say to Harry."

"I can imagine. I just got finished filling him and your lawyer, Zelman, in on the state of the investigation into Donny's murder."

Unlike with Harry, I had explained to Moe on the phone this morning about my looking into the case for the Starr Syndicate and their interests.

Moe said, "I spoke to Captain Chandler from Homicide. All smiles, Mr. Nice Guy. I did a drawing of Wonder Guy for his children. But he didn't fool me."

"Is that right?"

"He thinks *I* did this. Me, or *Harry* and me. I don't think he thinks Harry has the . . . this sounds bad . . . the brains to pull this off alone."

"I see."

The big eyes behind the glasses narrowed in concern. "You must understand—Harry is a sort of a genius. Do you know the term—idiot savant?"

"Yes."

But he defined his version of it anyway: "A simple soul with a God-given talent for something complex. Do you have any idea how *Wonder Guy* has changed the world?"

That sounded grandiose, but it wasn't really. In 1938, *Wonder Guy* had been just this oddball comic book on the fringes of newsstands. By early the next year, *Wonder Guy* was syndicated by Starr, growing quickly to a list of close to a thousand papers. By the end of '39, countless new superheroes and new comics publishers were on the stands, and by early 1940 *Wonder Guy* was a hit on the radio, and before long the animated cartoons, and . . .

"I didn't create *Wonder Guy*," Moe said. "Harry did. He may seem like an excitable boy, and he is, but always remember what he accomplished. Always remember his genius."

"You really are friends."

He sipped the hot coffee. "We are. We will be for life. I love him. He frustrates me, but what a gift he shared with his high-school buddy. Did you know, we both were left back a year?"

"I didn't."

"Jack, we were the butt of jokes. We were bullied, or were till I took that Charles Atlas course, anyway. I kind of muscled up, to defend the both of us."

I took a swig of Coke. "He was Ron Benson, mild-mannered radio reporter, and you were Wonder Guy."

"Don't kid yourself—we were both Ron Benson. We understand how a young boy feels, what kinds of things kids dream about. Flying. Being strong. Being loved by a pretty girl."

"You touched a nerve, all right."

He frowned, shook his head. "I'm afraid that dope Mortimer is going to screw it up. He keeps after us, Harry and me, to make the stories more real—make them scary, put more science fiction in, make the drawing less cartoony."

"Times change. Styles change. Is that why?"

He lifted one big shoulder. "I don't know. All I know is, the dream behind *Wonder Guy*—the dream of a lonely kid—is to be powerful and invulnerable, right? But you can't let the world know how bad you want it. You have to dream this dream with . . . with a light touch. They make it too serious, they screw it up. They lose the dream. Make it some kind of damn nightmare."

I'd known Moe a long time, or at least I'd met him a long time ago. He had never opened up to me like this. He'd always played a quiet second fiddle to Harry. And unlike Harry, Moe was clearly troubled by the death of Donny Harrison.

Quietly, not wanting any of his staff to hear, I asked, "Did you kill him, Moe?"

He shook his head. "I know I'm on the firing line. Even for all his smiles and excuse-me-for-intruding, Chandler asked questions that . . . that told me I was in trouble."

"About your diabetes. And the insulin."

He nodded gravely. Had another sip of coffee, then set cup and saucer on the scarred-up end table nearby. "Sure, I knew about Donny's diabetes, and the bottles he kept around and about. But putting poison in his insulin, anybody could've done that. Me having diabetes, and being familiar with the process of . . . what's that really mean?"

Again I said, "It's suggestive. It speaks to cops, and it speaks to juries."

"I suppose." The big eyes behind glass held me unblinkingly. "But I didn't do it. And Harry is the kind of guy who walks around an ant hill, if it's in his way. He's sweet. A goddamn little kid. And you know it."

I sighed. Swigged Coke. Said, "What I know is, there's no shortage of people who hated Donny Harrison. But maybe you know something, or have an instinct about who might—"

He gripped my arm with surprising strength. "Listen, Jack—I didn't hate Donny. What gets lost in the shuffle is how likable he could be. How . . . don't look at me like that . . . how *nice* he could be."

"Nice. Donny."

"Yeah. Donny. He and I had diabetes in common, right, everybody's making a big deal out of that. But he and I talked about it, sometimes. He was facing the same problems as me. He said he was going to pay for an operation on my eyes. Not take it out of my pay or anything, and when we started making noise about *Wonder Boy* and getting the *Wonder Guy* rights back . . . he took me aside and said, 'No matter how that goes, I gave you my word about that operation, and I stand behind it, pal.' Pal, he called me."

Behind the thick lenses, Moe's eyes had teared up.

If he'd ever been on my suspect list, I crossed him off then. When you're going blind, you don't bump off the guy who wanted to help you get your eyesight back.

Otherwise, Moe Shulman would have to do his dreaming like the rest of us—in the dark.

* * *

No one could deny the digs of both Harry Spiegel and Moe Shulman were those of successful men. But the *real* house that Wonder Guy built was on the north shore of Long Island, in the village of Kensington—the Tudor manor of Donny Harrison.

The Harrisons' world was one of tennis courts, golf courses, polo fields and yacht clubs, a heaven on earth for anyone with the right kind of money, even the sons and daughters of Jewish immigrants. Here the Harrison family could belong to a country club and attend cocktail parties and go to the synagogue on Old Mill Road.

I guided the convertible through the Victorian gates into the development, and soon had rolled up in front of the large home, a dozen rooms easy, with the typical Tudor thatched roof, side gables and decorative brown half-timbering on white stucco. Over the three-car garage was a sizeable loft with its own pitched roof—the living quarters chauffeur Hank Morella had mentioned.

And speaking of Morella, right now he was driving across the endless sloping lawn, and I don't mean in a car: bare-chested, he and his chinos and work boots were guiding a noisy power mower around, one of those new rotor jobs. The big, tanned, muscular lug might have been the model for Wonder Guy, or anyway the dumber looking knockoff, Marvel Man.

The walk was a curvy thing, with impeccably trimmed bushes all along (similar ones hugged the house), and I followed it like Dorothy on the Yellow Brick Road. I was halfway up when

Morella spotted me, shut off his noisemaker and strode over, frowning. His dark eyes were close enough together that this made him look even dumber, something I had until then not thought possible.

"What do you want around here, Jack?" he demanded, having to lean across the walk's knee-high hedge to do so. He had broad shoulders and a muscular chest, pearled with sweat and spattered with little grass bits, but he was breathing awful hard for a guy working a power mower.

"Hello, Hank," I said pleasantly. "I'm here to see Mrs. Harrison. She's—"

"Jesus, have a heart," he blurted, shoving his face in my face. "Don't you know she's grieving?"

I backed away. "You interrupted me, Hank. I was about to say she was expecting me."

"Oh. Really? She didn't say so."

"Are you her secretary, as well as chauffeur and yard boy?"

He swallowed, took a step back, looking embarrassed. "Sorry. I'm just . . . worried for her and the kids. It's awful hard on them, Mr. Harrison's tragedy."

By Mr. Harrison's tragedy, he meant Donny getting himself murdered.

"Haven't you been having people drop by a lot," I asked, "to pay their respects?"

I didn't know how religious Mrs. Harrison was, though the funeral had been Orthodox, and she could have been sitting shiva, which meant for seven days family and friends would drop by with food and comfort. Hell, she might have gone the full boat, with mirrors covered and sitting on the floor, and the men not shaving. You now know as much about Judaism as I do, since the major raised me to be about as Jewish as Bing Crosby.

"There have been a lot of callers," he said. "I didn't know you were paying your respects. I thought you were still nosing around about the, uh . . . you know."

I arched an eyebrow; somebody had to. "You don't think Mrs. Harrison might want to see her husband's killer caught, Hank?"

"I didn't say that! Look, I jumped the gun on you. I apologize. Go on up and knock. Her son and daughter are home—one of them will answer."

I held up a palm. "No offense taken, none meant. I know you and the family are close. You're staying on, then?"

"Sure. Of course . . . . Hey, I'm sorry, Jack. I'm on edge myself. If there's any way I can help with what you're trying to do, just, you know, say the word."

Something came immediately to mind.

"Actually there is," I said. I curled a finger and he came closer, and I damn near whispered. "Do you think Donny was aware that Miss Daily saw other men?"

"No! I don't think he had any idea."

"That sounds like you *did* know."

"Well . . . I heard things."

"Things like . . . names? I know Rod Krane and Honey were having an affair, until just recently. And I hear some bigwig at Americana was, too."

He was shaking his head; for the record, nothing rattled. "I can't imagine that. Mr. Cohn never fools around, and anyway, he and Mrs. Harrison are close friends; he would never betray her."

"I see."

"And I can't imagine Miss Daily wanting anything to do with Sy Mortimer."

"Me either." I ran through the names of some other top editors at Americana, and Hank shook his head at every one.

"Sorry, Jack. Wish I could be some help. And, uh . . . sorry about trying to give you the bum's rush. I was out of line."

I shrugged. "You're protective where the Harrisons are concerned. I respect that." I didn't really, but he seemed to like hearing it.

He went back to mowing.

The son answered the door—he was a short, slender if round-faced kid of maybe sixteen with more of his mom in his mug than his dad, and he wore a white shirt with a dark blue tie and light blue gabardine pleated slacks. The getup indicated he was the appointed doorman for those paying their respects. He didn't seem to be growing a mourning beard, but I wasn't sure he could have if he tried.

He ushered me through past some stairs—I glimpsed a very nicely appointed house in the French Provincial style, and noticed no covered mirrors—through a big white modern kitchen and out onto a brick patio.

Her round, nicely featured face a touch over madeup, Mrs. Harrison—in a loose black dress with white collar and cuffs—sat at a white round metal table on one of several white wire-metal chairs.

She smiled as I approached—the boy had disappeared—and started to get up, but I gestured for her to keep her place.

The handsome if stout woman was drinking lemonade, and a glass pitcher of the liquid and melting ice rested on a tray with half a dozen glasses awaiting drop-by guests like me. She poured a glass for me, and for several minutes—between sips—I paid my condolences, and spoke of how nice the service was, and heard about how a brother of Donny's had insisted on the Orthodox service, and she hadn't seen any reason why not.

"The major," I said, "thought the world of your husband."

She turned the dark blue eyes on me and, despite their expected filigree of red, they twinkled. "We spoke of the major, the last time I saw you."

"Yes." At the party. Right before Donny dove onto the cake knife.

"I sense that you . . ." She gave me a smile that granted forgiveness in advance. ". . . didn't share the major's view of Donny."

"Honestly, I didn't know him that well."

She gazed out into the yard, a beautifully manicured expanse of elaborate bushes with trees along either periphery. Not far from where we sat bloomed a flower bed of colorful perennials; a lattice gazebo perched halfway out. Birds, not informed Mrs. Harrison was in mourning, were chirping.

"He was not perfect, my Donny. But no man is. No woman, either. What do you think of Louie Cohn?"

"A cold fish," I said frankly. "But a hell of a businessman."

"Louie may think he's better off without Donny. He may consider Donny and Donny's style a thing of the past. But he's wrong. They were a team, a perfect team, and Louie will be half as effective without Donny."

"I can see that," I said. "Donny was quick, clever, lot of people liked him. Louie's the hardheaded, self-controlled partner."

"Yes. They were a perfect pair. Everybody loved Donny. Nobody loves Louie."

I guess I could have argued that somebody didn't love Donny, else he wouldn't have been murdered. But that might have lacked tact.

"Mrs. Harrison," I began.

She corrected me: "Selma."

"Selma. I know this is a very tough time for you. But I'm here for more than just expressing my sympathy."

She sipped lemonade. Raised one eyebrow, slightly. "Oh?"

"Maggie has me looking into Donny's death. His . . . I have to say it . . . murder."

She frowned, not critically, more in confusion. "Surely, that's a job for . . ."

"Wonder Guy?" I said with a smile. "No, not him, and not just the police. The man in charge, who you may have spoken to, Captain Chandler . . . ?"

"Yes. I spoke to him briefly, once on the phone, once here. He seems perfectly capable."

"I'm sure he is." I gestured with an open hand. "But the Starr Syndicate has business concerns at stake, and I know the people and the industry better than any Homicide Bureau cop. Maggie wants to make sure your husband's killer is brought to justice . . . and also wants to make sure no injustices are done."

"Injustices . . . such as?"

"Chandler is looking hard at the boys—Spiegel and Shulman. Moe is a diabetic, you know. Did Captain Chandler tell you . . . ?"

She nodded. "He explained that Donny's insulin was very likely tampered with. His people took bottles from our refrigerator in the kitchen, where you walked through."

"Yes." I drank lemonade; unlike the iced tea at the Spiegel apartment, this was just sweet enough. "With your permission, I need to bring up something painful."

Her smile was a knowing crease of amusement. "More painful than my husband's murder?"

"Possibly. May I proceed?"

"You may."

"His infidelity."

"You mean that Daily woman."

I wasn't surprised she knew: after all, she'd sent yard boy Hank over to pick up her hubby's things. And Honey insisted the other woman was aware.

"I do mean her," I said. "You've known a while?"

"For years."

"Did you . . . discuss it with Donny?"

"Never."

"When he announced he was having his birthday party at her suite, surely that must have . . . have . . ."

"Rankled?" An eyebrow went way up, but otherwise her expression remained impassive. "It was an indignity I had to bear. I told you, Donny wasn't perfect. He was a man. He traveled a lot, and there were many women. But only one wife. And he was a good husband. And a fine father."

I didn't know what else to ask. Surely she knew she was at least as prime a suspect as Spiegel and Shulman. Donny's insulin was in her kitchen, and he had died in his mistress's living room with his wife watching. Which most humiliated wives would find a perfect way to watch a cheating husband die.

So I asked the only question I had left: "Donny had more than his share of enemies, Selma. But do you suspect any one of them, in particular?"

She frowned at me, as if in shock. "Enemies? Donny didn't have an enemy in the world. If you're going to say mean things like that, Jack, I'll have to ask you to leave."

Damon Runyon called it Dream Street, a block's worth of Forty-seventh Street between Sixth and Seventh Avenues; but these days, nightmare was more like it. Two hundred yards of ratty hotels and ramshackle rooming houses where the owners of dreams-turned-to-dregs resided—grifters, horse players, dope addicts, pickpockets, washed-up vaudevillians, actors on the way down who were never very far up.

I made a point of calling on Will Hander, who roomed in this negative Valhalla, while the sun was still up, if barely. Not that you couldn't walk Dream Street at any hour—Broadway was just around the corner, the mink and pearls of Fifth Avenue one block east. The poor souls you encountered, in sunshine or neon, were no threat—peroxided old women walking their mutts; a panhandler seeking a quarter for "coffee"; a skinny streetwalker whose charms promised pleasure but boded penicillin. Here a bearded bum studied a scratch sheet on church steps; there a dipso sat in a doorway, shivering with something that wasn't cold, not on a late Saturday afternoon in July.

The danger, particularly after dark, was upstairs in the dismal, shabby buildings, in the ancient cubicles that passed for rooms, where vice of every stripe was available, from watered-down whiskey to hypos of H, from con games to crap games, from adulterous quickies to assorted versions of the Old Army game for sailors on leave of their senses.

Maggie had provided the address, and suggested I carry my gun. Unfortunately, "my" gun was the major's bulky Colt .45, brought home from the war before the last one; and none of my suits were cut to conceal it. And since my troubleshooter role had only recently gone private eye on me, I—unlike Bogart or Alan Ladd—had not got round to getting fitted for a shoulder holster.

So I went armed only with a sharp wit and the confidence of youth . . . and a roll of quarters, which made a nasty lump in the pocket of my lightweight suit jacket, but then could also make a nasty lump on anybody who gave me a problem, so call it a fair trade.

The stairs and walls hadn't seen paint since George M. Cohan was Broadway's fresh new face; they hadn't seen disinfectant, either, judging by the smell of urine, which was delicately laced with the bouquet of hotplate hash. But Hander was only three flights up, and I encountered no one on my climb. You might have thought the (what we'll charitably call) residential hotel was empty, if not for sounds behind closed doors, ranging from noisy bedsprings to hysterical laughter, with a shout of "Baby needs a new pair of shoes!" counterpointing the wail of an actual crying baby, to make the experience wholesome for the entire family.

I had tried to call Hander, but the only number Maggie had on the *Batwing* writer was a general one for the flophouse, and the three times I tried (right in a row), I got three different people who uttered three different expletives and hung up on me. None of them, apparently, Hander.

So once again I was dropping in unannounced. But on the third floor I realized I was in trouble—not danger, trouble. Hander was in Room 307, according to Maggie's info; but none of the doors had numbers. Well, some had numbers—for example, one said 6, another said 09 and another said 30, the remnants of once-proud three-digit designations fallen away like the sands of time (and flakes of paint).

I could really have used the help of a detective.

Anyway, I resorted to math, which I admit had been my worst subject, although considering the kind of all-around grades I racked up, the best wouldn't have been that encouraging, either. But figuring out that 09 had once been 309, and 6 had likely been 306, I thought Hander likely lived one door to the right of the latter.

This brilliant deduction was underscored by noise coming from behind that numeral-less door: typing.

A sound a writer makes. I smiled. Finally I had made my math teachers proud. . . .

I knocked and set free half a dozen or more little green chips of what a stickler would still call paint.

The typing continued.

I knocked again and dislodged more green dandruff.

The typing stopped.

"Will!" I said to the door. "It's Jack Starr—from the Starr Syndicate. Need a word!"

I heard a wooden chair squeal on a wooden floor, and hurried footsteps, then what I thought to be a drawer opening, and finally something glass go clunk. And a drawer slam shut?

Then the door opened and a guy who was maybe two steps above the bums on Dream Street below filled the space.

"Jack," he said, and grinned at me, like an old friend had just blown in. We'd met maybe three times.

Lanky, loose-limbed, Will Hander had a boyish face, despite the couple days' growth of beard, and a musical tenor. He looked forty breathing down fifty's neck, and was maybe thirty. His jet-black hair was curly, a full unruly head of it, and his bloodshot eyes added up to a patriotic red, white and blue. He was in a sweat-circled white shirt, sleeves rolled up, open at the throat showing black curly chest hair. His pants were lightweight and brown, and he was in his stocking feet. Something about him said he'd been an athlete once.

"Jack," he said. The smile took on an embarrassed edge. "You should've called."

"I tried. I talked to three of your secretaries, who all had physically impossible suggestions for me."

He laughed, a little too loud. "Yeah, this is a dump, and the clientele's a bunch of rummies."

Spoken with great conviction for a guy with liquor on his breath.

"Could I come in?" I asked. "My uncle lives down the hall, and if spots me, he'll want a five-spot."

Hander shook his head and laughed. "You are a cutup, Jack. You should write a strip for your stepmother."

Following him into the room, I said, "I don't think my sense of humor is ready for public consumption just yet."

Neither was Hander's apartment, if you could call it that.

One shabby little room, with an unmade single bed, a couple sheets and, folded at the foot, a threadbare blanket. The cracked walls were the color of chocolate, only not at all sweet. The furniture consisted of a cloth-covered wine-color couch and a green easy chair, both of whose cushion springs were making a break for it, and a battered dresser with a few water glasses on it and a smoky mirror over it.

A window on an alley was open, looking out onto a brick wall, but that was the source of air, which kept the box less than stuffy. In front of this scenic view, a black metal typing stand was set up, with a heavy oak wooden chair that had more scars than an over-the-hill boxer.

Hander, smiling big but the humiliation coming through, gestured me to the couch, and pulled his heavy typing chair away from the stand, whose two wings were spread, one holding a box of typing paper, the other its lid with script pages in it, another page curling in his portable Underwood.

We sat. The clunking sound I'd heard was him putting a bottle away, I figured. Judging by his breath, I'd say rye whiskey. And before you dismiss that deduction as one even Sherlock Holmes couldn't make, remember I was an MP in the war.

"I thought you lived out in the Bronx," I said, trying not to make it an accusation.

He folded his hands in his lap; slumped a little. Grinned like a kid caught playing with himself. "Yeah, I do. But, uh . . . a little family trouble."

"Sorry. None of my business . . ."

"No! No, that's fine. I got a beautiful wife and a beautiful kid, and sometimes . . . sometimes I fall off the wagon."

"I been there."

He gestured with open hands. "And Molly said, clean myself up. Looks bad in front of my boy."

"Sure."

His shrug was too big. "So I just burrowed in up here, to get ahead on some scripts."

"*Batwing?*"

"Yeah, *Batwing* and *Blue Barracuda* and some *Wonder Boy*. Mortimer likes my stuff. Keeps me alive, God bless him."

I shifted on the couch, trying to get comfortable. "Not everybody has kind words for Sy or, frankly, any of the higher-ups at Americana."

A smaller shrug. "Well, it's just a writing market for me. I freelance there and a few other places. Just, until . . . you know."

"Actually, I don't. Know what, Will?"

The half smile that came to the boyish mug was unforced. "Oh, this comics junk is just a means to an end. Just to get enough cash to keep the wife and kid afloat, till my ship comes in."

"What ship would that be?"

He laughed, and it was one of the worst laughs I ever heard.

"I'm like every writer—when I get ahead on freelancer work, I'm digging in on the Great American Novel."

I smiled. "Ah. Nobody's got around to writing that one yet, huh?"

"No, sir."

And here my money was on *Huckleberry Finn*.

"Not that I'm a snob," he said. "Some of the pulps, the better pulps, they have really good writing in them. That's where Chandler started. And Hammett. And lots of people."

Again I shifted on the couch, attempting to find an angle where my behind didn't receive unwanted acupuncture. "You had many pulp sales?"

"A few. It's just . . . comic books, that's a market I lucked into, and it's been a way to keep head above water."

I would question using any form of the word "luck" with a career choice that included this particular writer's garret. But that's just me.

"Having flat feet, being 1-A, was a kind of a break for me. So many in the business off to war, and not a lot of good comics writers around, if there is such a thing."

"It's a craft few can master," I said, meaning it. I saw the kind of submissions that came into Starr every day.

"You really think so?" He stood. "Say, can I get you a drink? I've been working all day, and I think maybe I could stand to wet my whistle."

"No, that's okay. I swore off the stuff for Lent."

He frowned at me, by the dresser now. "Aren't you Jewish?"

"Not very, but that was an attempt at a joke."

Now that my remark had been properly categorized, he laughed heartily, and opened a drawer and got out the rye whiskey bottle— I will pause for you to be impressed by my deductive skills—and filled one of the water glasses, halfway.

Dark bronze liquid sloshing in the glass (and probably in his stomach, too), Hander returned to the heavy, heavily scarred-up chair and sat. He sipped, obviously wishing for a gulp. Impressive self-control.

His smile turned serene. "What brings you around, Jack?"

"Missed you at Donny's funeral."

And now, finally, his expression darkened. "Yeah, well . . . I didn't suppose I was on the guest list."

"Not many artists or writers were there. Harry and Moe took a pass, too."

He was shaking his head. "I didn't hate the guy. I didn't wish him dead."

"Somebody did. Somebody who made that wish come true."

He'd been in the process of raising his whiskey glass to his lips when I said that, and my words actually interrupted that process. "You're not . . . looking into it, are you, Jack?"

"I am."

He looked at me like I'd just insisted the world was flat. "But the cops are doing that, aren't they?"

"Why, have you talked to Captain Chandler of the Homicide Bureau?"

He shook his head. "No, but I guess he went looking for me, all the way to the Bronx. I talked to Molly on the phone this morning, and she told me. But she hadn't given my address to him."

"To protect you?"

His previously chipper expression, however forced, had melted into hangdog despair. "No. So she wouldn't be embarrassed, when he saw where I . . . where I was staying, temporarily."

"Did she invite you back, then?"

His face bore the kind of sadness that tears just didn't do the trick for. "No. No, she's got it in her head that my drinking is out of control." His forehead tensed. "Jack, this is the first drink I've had, all day. I swear on my kid's head."

"Not my business, Will."

He sat forward, eyes glittering. "I mean, could a drunk turn out the scripts I do?"

Having read Hander's *Batwing* stuff—outrageous death traps and acrobatic fights interspersed with lunatic wisecracks often set in fun house–type settings with huge oversized props and looming grotesque faces—I'd have to say . . . hell, yes.

"No," I said. "Certainly not. But I heard you were trying to get some credit from Donny, for *Batwing*."

He held his free hand up, palm out, like he was swearing in, in court. "Look, I don't really give a damn about credit. Who cares if my name is on this crummy kid stuff? It'll only *hurt* me, right, when I'm doing serious novels? I want to *protect* my name, *save* my byline for when it *really* counts."

Yeah, and I heard Thomas Wolfe did all his comics stories anonymously, too. That, and as Tommy Fox.

I shifted again; come Monday, I was going to need a tetanus shot. "Then what had you been bugging Donny about, Will?"

"Money! Let Rod have his name all over the goddamn thing!

Do I want my next-door neighbors, out in the Bronx, knowing I created Sparrow and that stupid Harlequin? No way in hell . . . but I *do* want the dough I got coming to me. Did you know there's gonna be another serial! And all those toys. . . . Jack, do you realize I get standard freelancer money, same as anybody else, and it's me who *created* this garbage?"

Yes, his sense of pride was palpable.

I asked, "Why don't you talk to Krane about it?"

His face fell; shoulders, too. "I . . . I have, but . . . I have to be careful."

"Why?"

His expression was a frightened child's. "If I made Rod mad at me, really got on his bad side, don't you know what would happen? He'd stop using me as a writer. He'd pressure Americana not to use me. And, Jack, I got a family to support! Bills to pay!"

From these cracked-wall rat-trap surroundings, you'd have thought he had no more responsibility in life than the other alkies.

"So," I said, "you went to Donny."

"Right. Over and over again, I'd plead my case. And over and over again, he'd turn a deaf ear."

I frowned. "How'd you react to that?"

"Well . . . I didn't get mad. What good would that do? I understand that to a guy like Donny, business is business. I thought maybe I could wear him down. See, I was trying to appeal to his, you know, sense of fairness. Americana is the Wonder Guy company, right? Truth and justice and the American flag?"

"And how'd that work out?"

He shrugged, holding his hands palms up. "Look around you.

And now I'm left with Louie Cohn, who is about as compassion-ate as Himmler on a bad day. Let's face it, I made a lousy business deal, and I'm stuck with it."

I nodded. "Were you invited to Donny's birthday party?"

His face froze in a ghastly smile. "Me? No. Are you kidding? Maybe before I'd started making his life miserable with my re-quests."

Not demands. Requests.

"Did you know about Donny's diabetes?"

"Did Donny have diabetes?"

I tried another tack. "The party, it was held in his mistress's suite at the Waldorf. With his wife there."

"Ouch. Donny had a mistress, huh?"

"You really didn't know that?"

"No. Not that I'm surprised. Look, artists work up at Ameri-cana, sometimes—in the bullpen? Writers are just stuck in apart-ments and houses and what-have-you, sending in their scripts, getting their checks in the mail. I went up to Americana to see Donny, to try to get a fair shake out of him for *Batwing*, maybe half a dozen times over the years. Otherwise I never set foot."

I stood. "I better let you get back to it. Great American Novel and all that."

He stood, grinned sheepishly toward the sheet of typing paper curled in the Underwood. "I'm afraid, more like Tuxedo kidnap-ping Batwing's faithful valet, George, and sticking him on top of a giant wedding cake next to Feline. How it resolves, I have no idea."

"Ah. Well, finish your one drink of the day, and it may come to you."

He offered a hand to shake, and it was firm for a guy who refused to stick up for himself.

When I was down on the street, I was thinking what a good murder suspect Hander would have made, if only Rod Krane had been the victim.

Dusk had fallen—actually more than fallen, more like collapsed into night. Neons were painting the old gal that was Dream Street with their smeary rouge, and I guess I was distracted by the thought that I might have winded up in one of these doorways, myself, if I hadn't got off the sauce in the service, when the ham-size hand landed on my shoulder.

I was just starting to turn to see who it was when another big hand gripped my arm, and before I could say, "Pardon me," two guys had swept me off my feet and it wasn't love, ushering me into the nearby alley. The meager light from the street did nothing but wink off a few garbage cans, and I think I heard the scurry of rat feet when the two bigger rats slammed me against the brick wall and one of them stuck his face so close to mine, I could smell his Old Spice, though I doubted he was a sailor.

"Stay out of it," he growled. And it *was* a growl, an affectation really, and I wouldn't have been impressed if the other hadn't slammed a fist into my breadbasket.

That doubled me over, but I didn't throw up, and the hand on my left arm and another on my chest raised me back up against the brick, hard enough to rattle my teeth. The dimness of the alley kept them shapes, mostly, like fedora-sporting silhouettes in *Dick Tracy*, and everything about it was surreal, except the pain in my gut, which was very realistic indeed.

The other face got in mine and spat, "And stay away from her!"

Really spat, spittle all over my face, and somehow I anticipated the knee meant for my groin by lifting my own, my leg taking the brunt.

Then the other silhouette slammed a fist into my belly, but I was tensed this time, and I managed to slip my right hand in my suit jacket pocket and clutched the roll of quarters.

The guy at right let loose of my arm, maybe to work me over two-handed, and that was all the opening I needed. I punched him in the puss with the fist wrapped around the roll of coins, and damn near broke my hand, and certainly broke his nose.

He stumbled back into a shaft of light from the street and I could see twin streams of blood coming down from his nostrils; then I swung the same fist into the other one's gut to let him see how he liked it, which he didn't—he doubled over, lost his lunch, or maybe supper, and I took the opportunity to kick him in the ass. He threw an unintentional block into his buddy, who had staggered back to hold on to his bleeding face, and now went all the way down, with a whump.

I moved in on them, and slammed my fist into the puking one's side, and sent him down hard on the alley floor, and charged the guy with the bleeding face, who was on his feet again and backing up, mumbling for mercy but instead got clipped on the chin so hard that he tripped on his own feet and slammed into the opposite alley wall and slid down it to a sitting position, even as the roll of quarters burst and rained money on the pavement, little ting ting ting ting ting's, like a slot machine had paid off.

"Keep the change," I said, and got the hell out of there before they recovered.

I ran to Broadway and caught a cab and when the hackie asked, "Where to, bud? . . . Are you okay?" I said, "The Waldorf . . . never better."

The latter was a lie or at least an exaggeration, and the former was something my subconscious put in my mouth. I'd been busy just fighting back and surviving and triumphing and fleeing to think anything through, at least on the first floor of my brain.

But somewhere, the basement maybe, the gray matter had recognized those two, in the flashes of light from the street during the fight that had made them more than just silhouettes—they were goons with the Calabria outfit, Anthony something (they called him the Ant) and Carlo something (they called him Carlo).

And I knew that Frank Calabria often spent Saturday nights at the Waldorf, this time of year, when his wife was at their summer place and he was pretending he had business in town. Not every Saturday night, but a lot of them. I even knew where, if that were the case on this Saturday night, he'd have taken his sweetie.

In retrospect, you could argue I should have been paying more attention to the first floor than the basement. I didn't even go back to my apartment at the Starr Building to get the major's .45. And maybe I should have frisked those mugs and got their own guns off them, and questioned them, and taken their firearms and information away with me.

But I hadn't.

My instinct had been to run, and rarely when a human being has the instinct to run does it prove to be Mother Nature giving bad advice. Even on that stretch of Forty-seventh, cops would have soon entered the fray; and I was in no mood for cops. I wasn't sure what I was in the mood for, but it sure as hell wasn't for cops.

I wanted to beard that bastard Calabria in his den, for sending his goons to work me over, trying to scare me off the case. And if I was right about where he'd be right now, the prime minister of the New York underworld would be at his most vulnerable.

In the back of the cab, I checked myself over. My suit looked fine, no stains from the alley, neither garbage nor blood. My gut had taken the most punishment, and I was sore, but not as sore as I was in general about what Calabria had pulled. The only thing really scuffed up was my knuckles, which were skinned and bloody, and I held a handkerchief over them. By the time I got dropped at the Park Avenue entrance of the Waldorf, the bleeding had let up.

Big Jim and his putty-faced pal were seated in the lobby again, but I made sure they didn't see me as I took a circuitous, periphery-hugging route to the special elevators to the Starlight Roof.

I moved quickly through the biggest, most exclusive room in the city, so as not to be stopped with such embarrassing questions as *Do you have a reservation, sir?* or *Where do you thinking you're going?* The exquisite chamber, with its vast grill-like ceiling and large, gleaming sky-blue stars, was a blur—the bandstand with Cugat in white dinner jacket and orchestra in gold-trimmed royal blue, the couples in evening dress on the endless dance floor doing the samba, columns and pilasters, stair railings displaying boxed flowers, huge antique gold mirrors making the big room huge, mosaic walls of forest creatures including a bird of paradise. . . .

Calabria was up a level from the dance floor, tucked away

between pillars, at a table for two with his brunette mistress, a former showgirl who at thirty was still an eyeful. They had apparently already eaten, as they were drinking the Starlight Roof's fifty-cent coffee and sharing a plate of the buck-fifty cheesecake. Even the criminals were getting robbed at those prices.

His first response was to smile in surprise on seeing me, which I admit threw me a little. That somehow not unattractive reptilian pan of his should have frowned or even flinched, however barely. Could Calabria be that cold-blooded? Could a guy he'd just fingered for a beating walk in, and still raise from him the perfect calculated, calibrated reaction?

I took a spare chair from a nearby table and diners with big eyes and outraged expressions were staring and waiters in white livery were closing in on me like the cops on Bonnie and Clyde, when Calabria—he was in a black pin-striped suit with a dark blue tie against a pale blue shirt, very dapper—held up a benign hand, a traffic cop signaling stop, still smiling but thoughtful now.

The waiters receded, and I sat.

The brunette seemed bored, much more interested in her cheesecake than in this rude intruder. She had the kind of cartoonishly beautiful features that look great from the audience but faintly grotesque close up. She wore a sleeveless dark blue satin evening dress and that showed off her chest without being obnoxious about it.

Under the big lumpy nose, an upper lip curled in what would have to be termed a smile. "You seem tense, Jack."

"Kind of."

He gestured with a thick-fingered hand, magnanimously; his

cuff link was a silver FC. "You want something to drink? Coke or Seven-Up or something? I know you're off the hard stuff."

"No, thanks."

He shrugged; the shoulders of the suit were padded, which with his fullback's frame was redundant. "I don't mean to be a bad host or nothin'. But you mind me asking if you're gonna make a habit of busting in on me, uninvited? First the barbershop, now bargin' in on my private life right out in public and everything."

I may have smiled; couldn't swear to it. "I got to hand it to you, Frank. You do have your nerve."

He grinned and his eyebrows hiked. "*I* have nerve. Kid, you must have ice water in your veins." He leaned toward me and the eyes in particular were reptilian. "Give me a reason not to open you up and see for myself, why don't you?"

I may have laughed; couldn't swear to it. "You even *hired* me. Why would you do that? Promise me ten grand, and then send two goons to scare me off."

"Two who to what?" His brow furrowed; the confusion looked genuine. Was he that good? "Settle down, Jack. I can see you are upset. Upset people make misjudgments. They get themselves in all kinds of unnecessary spots."

I leaned in. My eyes were tight and so was my voice. "You didn't just send that gorilla Anthony, what do they call him, the Ant . . . and that moke Carlo . . . to work me over?"

His glare of a frown would have killed every snake on Medusa's head. "Don't insult me in front of the doll, kid."

The doll was eating cheesecake.

I showed him my scraped knuckles. "If I hadn't had the foresight to carry a roll of quarters with me, those two would've made marinara out of me, Frank."

He gripped my wrist. Hard. Fingers clutching just under the hand with the nasty knuckles.

I just looked at him.

And he looked at me. "I swear on my friendship with the major, I never sent those sons of bitches." He let go of my wrist and shook his head. "The Ant and Carlo, those jackasses ain't worked for me in years. Not since they boosted those ration books out of that warehouse in '43, the disloyal unpatriotic bastards. Some things you just don't do."

I sat back. Blinked. "They . . . they don't work for you. Haven't worked for you for . . ."

Again he shook his head, forcefully. "No. I am not handing you a line, Jack. Do I *need* to hand you a line?"

". . . No."

"And I'm not." He shrugged rather grandly. "Somebody else must've sent them."

"Who?"

A less grand shrug. "I got no idea."

But I did.

I *knew*, and it excited me and made me sick at the same time.

I got to my feet. "I'm sorry, Frank. I'll apologize later. In detail and abject as hell, I promise."

"Kid . . ."

But I was gone, moving fast in and around waiters and patrons and out of rhythm with Cugat's conga as the Starlight Roof again blurred past me, even more indistinct.

I had to take the elevator down to the lobby to grab one of the tower ones, and it was frustrating, going down to go back up again, frustrating as hell. You might ask what my rush was, and I can't explain. Nothing logical. Some pieces had come together in my mind, and the picture of a killer had been assembled. That picture didn't necessarily mean anything other than I had identified the party behind Donny Harrison's death.

But I had a sick, shuddering feeling that it might mean more.

When I got to her door, it yawned open.

I didn't even bother to call out. Somehow I had the presence of mind to bump it open with my shoulder, wide enough to enter, not disturbing any prints. Funny how part of you can be detached, and another part out of control.

And I didn't even move that quickly when I saw her, as somehow I knew I would see her, on that emerald sofa where we'd sat and talked and flirted and kissed and finally argued, last time I saw her.

She wore the same black dressing gown I'd seen so often, with the same touches of pink here and there, ribbon and flesh, and I've wondered if I might have saved her if I'd moved faster, if I hadn't suddenly been walking slow-motion in sand, if a Walcorf doctor could have rushed there and done something, but from the emptiness in her wide eggshell blue eyes and the paleness of her face and the horrible, unspeakable loll of her tongue from her blue lips and the chilling overall sprawled stillness of her, I knew I'd dropped in on Honey Daily, unannounced, for the last time.

My first call—made from the darkened bedroom, sitting on the edge of her bed with its blue satin tufted headboard and matching blue satin bedspread—was to the hotel manager, who I filled in quickly and the on-staff doctor would be immediately dispatched. I said I'd take care of notifying the police.

And, by all rights, my next call should have been to the Homicide Bureau or even to the general police emergency number. But I called Maggie instead. I tried her apartment phone, figuring the odds were good she'd be in—she wasn't quite out of her reclusive phase, after all—and indeed I got her, on the third ring.

"Maggie," I said, "I'm at Honey Daily's suite."

Quickly I described finding the body, and said, "I killed her, didn't I?"

She knew what I meant; it was in her voice when she calmly

replied, "Nonsense. You keep that kind of talk away from the police. *Jack?* I want to hear you say it."

"I won't be dumb," I promised.

"I'll be right over."

"Maggie, you don't need to—"

But she'd hung up.

I'd believe it when I saw it, Maggie Starr, still not at her fighting weight, setting foot in public. And what the hell good could she do here? If she could even get in. This was a crime scene.

My odds of finding Chandler in the office on a Saturday night were much worse, but maybe I had just a tiny bit of luck coming, because he was there. A gang fight between a bunch of kids on the lower east side, with switchblades and zip guns, had kept him working overtime. He was on his way out the door when my call caught him.

"I don't have to tell you not to touch anything," Chandler said.

"Only thing I've touched is this phone I'm using. Bedroom phone."

"Good. Do me a favor. That hotel doc should be there any second. He may not have dealt with a crime scene before. Give him the rundown."

"Okay."

"And if you feel he's trustworthy, leave him to it and step out into the hall and stand guard till I can get some uniforms up there. I'll get on that right now, and then hit the siren and be there."

"Siren's not necessary. She's not going anywhere."

Neither was I.

I followed Chandler's orders. When the doc came—a slight, balding, bespectacled guy under forty, hauling a black bag and wearing a black suit, looking more like an assistant mortician than a physician—I asked if he'd worked a crime scene before. He said no. I said when he'd determined the corpse was a corpse—and I knew this would take no time at all—he needed to make sure he didn't touch or disturb anything. He said fine.

He knelt near her—a small enough man that he could do that without moving the coffee table—and spent maybe thirty seconds before standing and giving me that look-cum-head-wag that is the most easily understood diagnosis a doctor can make.

"We need to get out of here," I said. "Make room for the cops and the coroner's people."

"They'll want to talk to me." He got a card from his inside suitcoat pocket. "I'll be in my office. It's on the first floor, next to Cook's Travel Service."

Then he and his black suit and black bag went off down the hall, toward the elevator, and I stood with my back to the wall, next to the ajar door, and waited.

I can't tell you how much time passed before the two uniformed men arrived—not long, maybe ten minutes. They'd got the word from Chandler via radio. One of them took over my position by the door in the hall. The other one was checking the apartment out, not touching anything, opening doors with elbows, making sure no other bodies were waiting to be discovered, and no killers were hiding out in closets or under furniture.

I followed him into the kitchen. I'd already explained who I was, that I'd found the body and called Captain Chandler.

"He's going to want to talk to me," I said.

This copper was about fifty and had seen everything; this probably wasn't even his first dead strangled beautiful woman. And his matter-of-fact manner was wholly called for.

That didn't mean I had to like him.

He said, "Yes, the cap's gonna want to talk to you," like he was dealing with a child.

"Do you have any objection to me waiting in the bedroom?"

He was checking inside the refrigerator, opening it by using the end of his nightstick. I would have paid anything to have somebody jump out at him. But it was the same old mostly empty fridge that she'd made me that terrific breakfast out of.

He frowned at me like I was a bug buzzing him. "Why don't you stay out in the hall with Officer Davis?"

"I made the call from the bedroom. I was a friend of Miss Daily's, and I'd prefer to be by myself. I need a moment. You mind?"

He frowned at me, harder. "I think the hall would be better."

A cop like that can be a problem. He's the superior officer of the young uniform; but otherwise he takes orders. His decision-making skills are limited.

"I'll be in the bedroom," I said, and shouldered my way out.

I did not look at the sprawl on the couch that was Honey. I quickly walked past the Donny-size stain into the darkened bedroom and sat on the edge of the bed by the phone and faced the drawn curtains and tried to let the shadows swallow me up. If you were thinking I angled my way into the bedroom so I could do some inspired detective work, you'd be wrong. I just wanted to be alone.

Of course I had plenty of company—my thoughts, and my self-recriminations. You've been reading this, not living it, so you have probably been ahead of me for some time. But I honestly did not know who had killed Donny—and, now, Honey—until Frank Calabria nudged the facts and circumstances into place.

Maggie knew. I could tell from her voice. She was ahead of me. And she didn't even have access to any of what I'd learned today.

Maybe I sat there and wept a while. I'm not saying I did. But it would have been appropriate behavior, as far as I'm concerned, even for a war vet with a Silver Star.

Finally I heard Chandler and what must have been a small army of technicians—lab guys, photographer, coroner's man—troop in. That older uniform must have told Chandler where I was, because after less than a minute with Honey's remains, he entered the bedroom.

He stood framed in the doorway, another silhouette in a fedora, the illumination of the living room behind him. "You mind if I turn the lights on?"

"Not the overhead," I said. "A lamp, maybe."

He came over and switched on the nightstand lamp on the other side of the bed, behind me. To my back, he asked, "What are you doing in here, Jack?"

Looking at nothing, I said, "Staying out of the way."

He came around and stood in front of me, the draped window at his back. He was in a blue suit with a lighter blue tie loose around his neck. He pushed the fedora way back on his head, and loomed over me, a big good-looking blond leading man, the kind of guy who wouldn't have made mush out of a case like this, like I had.

"Tell me," he said.

"Really, I told you everything on the phone."

"That was *Reader's Digest*. Give me the unabridged."

I'd been seen in the hotel—my entrance and exit upstairs at the Starlight Roof could hardly have been more dramatic—so I told him most of it. Said I'd been jumped by some guys who I recognized as Calabria goon squad, and came here to the hotel to confront the big boss, on the off chance he was dining with his mistress, which had proved to be the case.

"Go on," he said, his tight voice going well with the narrowed eyes.

I shrugged. "Not much more to it than that. Calabria said he'd fired that pair years ago, over some ration books they boosted. Seems Frank considers himself a loyal American. All I know is their first names—Anthony and Carlo. You might be able to get more out of Calabria, good citizen that he is."

His head moved to one side. "What made you come down and check on Miss Daily?"

"Who said I was checking on her?"

"Impression I got."

"Didn't mean to lead you astray, Captain. I was here, at the hotel, so I decided to drop in on her."

His hands went to his hips, elbows winged out. "You knew her well enough to do that?"

"I met her at Donny's birthday party. If you look that up in your notes, you'll see it's the one he dropped dead at."

"Yes," he said dryly, "I recall."

"Anyway, we hit it off, Miss Daily and me. I saw her a couple times since."

His head straightened back up, and his chin lifted, as if daring me to clip it. "Were you intimate?"

"Do you mean did I ever sleep with her?"

"Yeah. I mean did you ever sleep with her."

"That's a little personal, isn't it?"

"Yeah. Very goddamn personal. Did you?"

"I said we were intimate. That doesn't have anything to do with anything."

His smirk stopped just this side of offensive. "Why don't you let me decide that one for myself, Jack. You've been poking around, haven't you? The Harrison murder?"

"I've been asking a few questions." I gestured with an open hand. "You're aware I'm a licensed private investigator. And I'm looking out for the Starr Syndicate's interests in the case."

The eyes narrowed again. "What interests would those be?"

"Talent that might or might not be involved in the murder."

"Only now it's murders."

"Yes. I know. Check your notes again—I found her."

He drew in a big breath and let it out slow. "You know, Jack, you don't strike me as quite as funny, in this context. Context of a dead woman you were intimate with, I mean."

"Do I look like I'm busting out laughing?"

"You're not crying."

"Would you like me to?"

He was staring at me; no other word for it. "Who have you spoken to, in the last few days, regarding the Harrison murder?"

I told him.

"Have you found anything out that might be pertinent to the investigation?"

I shrugged. "I wouldn't know, unless you shared what you've learned with me. I'm sure you're a much better investigator than I'll ever be. I can't imagine I'd find out anything that—"

"Then why are you bothering?"

"Bothering . . . ?"

He glared. "Bothering looking into the Harrison murder, if you have so much *confidence* in me."

Another shrug. "I know the comics business. I know the people. That might give me an edge."

He took a step forward, which made him really loom. "Do you know that happens to licensed investigators who withhold evidence?"

"They aren't licensed anymore?"

"Bingo. But they don't need to be licensed; not required in jail."

I sighed. "Look, don't you have a crime scene to deal with? You and I could sit down, some time tomorrow maybe, and we could compare what we've learned." I shook my head. "How can I know if I'm withholding anything, if I don't know what you've got?"

An eyebrow hiked. "You could tell me what you've found."

"I've found a platoon of people with good reasons to want Donny Harrison dead."

"Which of them might also have wanted Miss *Daily* dead?"

"That," I said, "is the pertinent question."

"Care to make a selection?"

". . . I'll get back to you."

His affability was all used up. His expression was a sneer, a frustrated one, but a sneer. "How would you like to be locked up as a material witness?"

"That one I can answer, Captain. No." I nodded toward the living room. "What do you think of that stain on the floor?"

He frowned, glanced that way despite himself, then focused on me and said, "*You're* asking the questions, now?"

"An honest exchange of ideas and information between two professional investigators with a mutual interest in solving a case."

"Don't bullshit a bullshitter, Jack."

"What about that stain, Captain?"

His frown deepened with frustration. "What about it? Blood, perspiration, dye from the costume."

"Is that what your lab told you?"

He shook his head. "We didn't make a lab test. When something is that obvious, why would you?"

"Give me a second while I memorize that . . . never too late to learn."

Chandler started counting on his fingers before he realized he could only use up one. "Harrison had recently injected himself with insulin, which we believe to have been spiked with an organophosphate."

"Believing isn't knowing. Not unless you consider police work a religion and not a science."

He glowered. "What's your point, Jack?"

"Make a lab test of threads from that area in there. Not too late."

"If you know something—"

But I didn't. The truth was, I hadn't seen the results from the Hirsch lab yet.

That older uniform stuck his head in. "Captain! There's a woman out here who wants to be let in. Says she's with your witness. A Miss Starr."

I grinned up at him. "Now's your chance. Be sure to tell her how her pinups warmed you up through lots of hard nights in the Pacific."

He flicked a frown at me, but told the uniform, "Show her in here. Be nice."

Chandler took his fedora off and a few moments later the impossible happened: Maggie Starr had broken her hibernation to come to my aid. She filled the doorway, looking beautiful but businesslike in a white dress with a black jacket, the latter decorated with a jeweled rose appliqué, a small black purse in her white-kid-gloved hands. She wore a small black hat, tilted, and was in full battle-array makeup, big green eyes highlighted and her kiss of a mouth a deep, rich red.

I sometimes forgot how tall she was, until I saw her out in public. But she had a commanding, even charismatic air about her.

"Captain Chandler," she said, her rich contralto filling the room without trying. "Jack has mentioned you. He seems to have a great deal of respect for you."

"He's done a good job of hiding it, just now," Chandler said on his way over to her, but his tone was friendly. "Jack's probably told you I'm a big fan. It's a pleasure to finally meet you, despite the circumstances."

She offered her gloved hand and, after a moment, he took it and shook. What was he trying to do, figure whether to kiss it or not?

"Yes," she said, stepping past him into the room, "we might have found a better way. But this is the way that we have—do you know who did this, Captain?"

She moved to a new position, not deep into the room, but enough to make him tag after her.

"No," he said. "Obviously we think it may be related to the Harrison murder, but it's far too early to say."

She raised an eyebrow. "You *do* know that Miss Daily had a number of boyfriends beside Mr. Harrison?"

"No. Actually, we didn't. Don't."

"Ah." She smiled at him, the way a queen does to a minor underling—a jester, maybe. "Then, based upon what Jack has reported to me . . . about his inquiries? He may have come upon a number of things that you haven't."

I was enjoying this, from my perch on the edge of the bed, across the room from them. I had to twist my torso to see it, but it was worth it.

"Yes," Chandler said, playing awkwardly with his hat in his hands, "Jack and I have been discussing that."

"May I make a suggestion?"

"By all means!"

"Will you, or your people, be working tomorrow, Sunday, on this case?"

"I probably will be, yes. Certainly my men will be on it. Murder doesn't get any days off."

"No. Murder doesn't stand on ceremony at all." She flipped a gloved hand. "What I would suggest is that you sit down with Jack, either at our office . . . and Sunday is not a problem for us, we live in the same building as where we work . . . or at the Homicide Bureau. He'll share everything he's found."

He was holding the fedora to his stomach now, as if protecting a wound. "We could do it right now . . ."

"No, Captain Chandler, I think you should run along and conduct this important investigation. You have a dead woman in the other room, after all, and from what the doctor I spoke to—"

"You spoke to *what* doctor . . . ?"

"I stopped by the Waldorf doctor before I came up. You'll be speaking to him, I'm sure, since he was the first physician to attend to the body."

"Yes, we, uh . . ."

"And he said he believed the murder had happened shortly before Jack arrived—within an hour, at the outside. Of course, that's a preliminary judgment, and your crack people, the coroner's crew and your forensics team, they'll put a button on it, I'm sure."

"Yes. Yes, they will."

She beamed at him and picked some lint off his left shoulder. "So. With a fresh corpse and a fresh murder scene, why waste your time on Jack, much less me? . . . What has your lab said about that stain in the other room?"

Chandler flashed a look at me. Not angry. More like an animal crossing the road that just heard a big sound that was about to turn out to be a truck. "Well, uh . . . I don't believe we've checked it yet."

"I realize that's one whole murder ago, but you might want to. I think the results might be interesting."

"Yes." He was gazing at her suspiciously, as if her buried sarcasm had just stuck its head up at him and thumbed its nose. "Well, I will do that."

"Good."

He grinned at her, a pretty "aw shucks" expression for such a hard-boiled Manhattan dick. "And, really, Miss Starr, it's a pleasure to finally meet you."

"I know. . . . Do you mind if I sit with Jack for a moment? We'll clear out very soon. Long before you get around to checking this room out."

"Yeah. Uh, sure. Go ahead. Try to be out of here in . . . fifteen minutes?"

She beamed at him again and touched his arm. "Less. . . . Now get to work! You have a killer to catch."

He grinned like a kid and went out and for a minute I thought she might give his butt a paddle.

She shut the door and came over and sat beside me. She slipped an arm around me. She'd never done that before.

"Are you all right?"

My nostrils took in her perfume, one of her favorites: My Sin. "I guess I've been better. Kind of in shock."

She glanced toward the door. "Captain Chandler seems all right. Civil servants aren't the most imaginative people in the world, and he was a little flummoxed at meeting me." Her laugh was a throaty purr. "You know, if these little boys have played with themselves, while thinking of you? You can get anything you want out of them."

I gave her a horrified sideways look. "I really didn't need to know that, Maggie."

She shrugged. "New information. Having new information, more information, is always beneficial . . . which is something the good captain hasn't grasped yet."

"You *know*, don't you?" I said.

"Yes."

"So you get why I blame myself, then."

"I do." She shook her head. "But it's a load. The blame is the killer's, and the killer's alone."

I shook my head. "But how could *you* know? When I finally, stupidly, put it together, hell . . . it was after a full day of interviews, and—"

She slipped a gloved hand over my mouth to silence me.

Then she got into the little black clutch purse and took out a folded piece of green paper. Handed it to me.

I had a look: the results from the Hirsch lab.

"Leo Hirsh," she said, "ran it over to me this afternoon. They work Saturday mornings, you know. And I think he saw this as his chance to get an autographed picture. And I gave him a good one. More skin than I usually serve up."

"Please," I said irritably, as I read the thing over. "There were traces of perspiration, but . . . Maggie, that stain out there, it's soaked with that stuff, that organophosphate jazz."

She made an affirmative hum and smiled doing it. Then: "How does that fit in with your thinking?"

"It turns it around a little . . . but still a perfect fit. Forgive the pun."

Not much of a pun, but if you understand it, you know who the killer is.

She smiled some more. "I like puns. You never have to ask me for forgiveness for a good pun. Where would the monologue I did, with my striptease, be without some choice double entendres?"

I was gaping at her. "So what do we do? Do we give this to Chandler?"

She waved at the air with a gloved hand. "Christ, we already have. You and I both did everything but bend him over that stain and rub his face in it."

I studied her but it didn't get me anywhere. "What do you have in mind, Maggie?"

"Something." Her free hand clasped mine; despite the glove, it was a startlingly personal gesture, and another first. "Jack, my only fear is what you might do if you got your hands on that. . . . Will you *promise* me you won't do anything rash?"

"Why?"

Her mouth smiled but her eyes frowned. "Normally when you ask someone not to do something rash, Jack, the response isn't 'why.' I don't want any vigilante nonsense. Understood?"

"Understood."

She turned toward the draped window and stared, thoughtfully. "But I think I would take great satisfaction in bringing this person to justice. How about you?"

"Oh yeah."

"Good. Then we're in agreement."

I was shaking my head. "But Chandler is talking pretty tough, Maggie. Withholding evidence, stripping me of my license, me or even *us* getting jailed as material witnesses. . . ."

She held up a white-gloved hand: stop. "We won't withhold anything. We can even tell him who our suspect is."

"Suspect! Not a suspect, there's no doubt that—"

"No, but there may not be enough evidence for Chandler to make an arrest. I propose we cooperate with him, and give him, oh . . . all the way to Monday evening to make an arrest. If he hasn't managed that, then we will have to do something about it."

"Like what?"

"Like," she said, shrugging, "get a confession."

"WAS THE PRIME MINISTER OF THE UNDERWORLD DISPLEASED WITH HIS SILENT PARTNER IN THE COMICS GAME?"

"DID **LOUIE COHN** CONSIDER HIS PARTNER-IN-CRIME-COMICS A LIABILITY? OR WAS **HONEY DAILY** LOUIE'S LA AMOUR?"

"WAS **ROD KRANE** AFRAID DONNY WOULD CREDIT THE OTHER MAN BEHIND **BATWING?** OR WAS HE JEALOUS OF HONEY'S **OTHER** HONEYS?"

"WAS SPIEGEL — AND/OR SHULMAN — DETERMINED TO HAVE TRUTH, JUSTICE AND DONNY, OUT OF THE WAY?"

"HAVE WE 'FRAMED' THE RIGHT KILLER IN THESE PANELS? OR IS THE PICTURE OF SOMEONE ELSE? SELMA HARRISON PERHAPS, OR FAMILY CHAUFFER HANK MORELLA?"

"OR MAYBE WILL HANDER, OR SY MORTIMER?... AT LEAST ONE OF THIS PARADE OF NOT-SO-COMIC CHARACTERS IS A **MURDERER.**"

Business at the Strip Joint on Mondays was almost always slow, and Maggie and Felix, the manager, had been kicking around staying open Sundays instead. So it was no great sacrifice for Maggie to close the restaurant for a private party, though I'm sure the guests were startled to find the restaurant empty but for a handful of waiters and waitresses.

The group had been invited, each by a personal phone call from Maggie Sunday evening, to attend a business dinner Monday night, which would be on the Starr Syndicate's tab. She had invited nine, and only one—attorney Bert Zelman—had a conflict that couldn't be broken. That was okay, because he wasn't really a suspect.

Not that the other guests had any idea that they were attending as suspects—all the invitees had at least a tenuous tie to the Starr Syndicate, enough to make a business dinner invite like this one credible.

Three smaller tables had been arranged into one long one, fairly close to the wall on which numerous comic strip characters had been drawn (and colored) in grease pencils. This particular stretch of the wall was mostly Starr Syndicate properties, and was no doubt why Maggie had instructed the Strip staff to set the banquet-style seating up here, so that Wonder Guy (a large drawing in full flight) and Batwing (a crude but recognizable sketch actually drawn by Krane himself) would loom over us.

I say us, but I was not at the table. I sat on a stool at the end of the bar, just a trifle kitty-corner from the table, though well in earshot. Next to me sat chauffeur Hank Morella, who Maggie had invited inside rather than have him wait at the curb for Selma Harrison.

Hank was back in his chauffeur livery, gray, not green this time, with the cap on the bar; he was having a beer and I was having a Coke on ice. Or a rum and Coke, no rum, as I'd described it to Honey Daily, what seemed a thousand years ago and was only four days.

Everybody was drinking, the Strip Joint barmaids (in their white shirts, black bow ties and tuxedo pants) keeping everyone's glass full. No actual food, not even a snack had been served, and the guests looked like they might any time start eating the red-cloth rose arrangements in two good-size centerpieces. The distinctive and decidedly pleasant aromas of the restaurant's kitchen provided convincing evidence that food would, eventually, be served.

On the far side of the table—with Wonder Guy and Batwing drawings looking over their shoulders—were, left to right: Will Hander, in a brown suit with a brown-and-yellow tie, shaved, not looking like a guy who lived in a flophouse, rye whiskey, no rocks; Sy Mortimer, in an off-the-rack blue suit with a red bow tie, beer; Louie Cohn, in a black suit with a black bow tie, looking like he couldn't decide whether he wanted to be a maitre d' or an undertaker when he grew up, gin fizz; and Selma Harrison, in a black-and-white print dress with a white collar, like she was gradually moving out of mourning, Chablis.

The three on the other side—Harry Spiegel and Moe Shulman, in off-the-rack brown suits, drinking beer, and Rod Krane, again with the white dinner jacket, martini—would've had their backs to me, but I had profile views: their chairs were angled to face the head of the table, the end closest to me, where Maggie right now was standing to address the group.

She was in full battle array now, all right. Her makeup stopped short of being more appropriate for the stage than real life, her green eyes longer-lashed than God intended, her freckles hiding under face powder, her lips a scarlet red, with a beauty mark on her right cheek that also wasn't the Almighty's idea.

Her dress was striking, a Maggy Rouff design from her most recent London trip—pale smoke-gray crepe with pushed-up sleeves and a double-pointed peblum with a darker gray big-buckled belt. She wore black gloves that went halfway to her elbows, like something D'Artagnan misplaced. Her red hair was full and to her shoulders (a wig but a damn fine one), no hat, with a small jeweled broach depicting her trademark red roses. Definitely at her fighting weight, she looked elegant and sexy and—despite the friendly smiles and warm comments she was tossing like a flower girl dispensing petals at a wedding—dangerous.

Maggie was drinking, too, of course—a Horse's Neck. Or that's what she would be drinking, if she ever got around to it. I noticed the glass had not yet touched her lips.

No need for her to ping a water glass to get attention—once she'd risen in her full glory the guests turned to her, hushed. They were smiling. She was, after all, a celebrity, and being in her presence felt special.

Tonight it should feel particularly special.

As she stood beaming out over grateful subjects, as if they were a particularly responsive first-night audience, she said, "First I want to thank you all for coming at such short notice. But I must admit I've gathered you together on something of a false pretense . . ."

Guests exchanged glances; then murmuring was halted by her raised black-gloved palm.

". . . but you needn't worry. You will be rewarded with the finest strip steak in New York, and at the expense of the Starr Syndicate, in gratitude for your presence, and your continued efforts on the behalf of the comics business."

A leering Rod Krane said, "You're not trying to get me liquored up again, are you, Maggie?"

"No. I find you rarely need encouragement, Rod."

This got an appreciative laugh from most of the group, though you had the feeling Will Hander, staring blankly at his *Batwing* co-creator, didn't find anything about Rod Krane all that amusing.

Harry Spiegel, fidgeting like a kid in the backseat on a car trip waiting for the next bathroom stop, almost shouted, "Freelancers like us don't mind a free meal, Maggie—but what's this about, anyway?"

Her smile remained but had lessened its voltage; her eyes traveled from face to face. "Some of you . . . certainly *one* of you . . . have already guessed. The business of this meeting is not comics. It's murder."

A symphony of chair squeaks and clothing rustle and whispers followed, and she raised high a hand that might have been in benediction, but wasn't.

"You've all seen the papers," she said. "It's taken till today, but the coverage has finally gotten brutal. Another murder will do that, particularly when . . . meaning no disrespect, Selma, not wanting you to be uncomfortable, dear . . . when the second victim was the mistress of the first victim."

Indeed the headlines today had screamed (except for the *Times*, which merely insisted) that *Wonder Guy* publisher Donny Harrison's death by poisoning had been confirmed by "officials" as a murder; and that the strangulation slaying of Honey Daily, Harrison's "kept woman," was believed by the police to be related.

The papers had nothing about any significant developments in the case (or cases), but that wasn't bad reporting, simply Captain Chandler and the rest of the Homicide Bureau not getting anywhere. I had spent three hours back in Chandler's office, tearing the heart out of a lovely Sunday afternoon, telling him everything I knew, including who I suspected.

And Chandler had agreed with my (and Maggie's) conclusions, but did not have enough physical evidence to support taking the theory to the district attorney.

At the head of the table, my tall lovely stepmother hovered over her guests and now no trace of smile remained; her arms were folded, and she might well have been the bailiff in a court-room, or at least in a courtroom in a Minsky's sketch.

"From the start," she said, "Donny's murder seemed directly related to the comic-book business—he even died wearing a Won-der Guy costume. . . . By the by, Selma, how many of those did Donny have?"

Startled, the plump, pretty widow said, "Why . . . just the one. He had a few Wonder Guy T-shirts he would wear . . . he liked to unbutton his shirt at parties and say, 'This looks like work for Wonder Guy!' "

A real cutup, our Donny.

"But," Selma was saying, "he just had that one special cos-tume that he wore at events like conventions and big sales meet-ings and, you know, things."

"Of course," Maggie said, not unkindly, "you had a reason for resenting your husband that really had nothing to do with comics. He was unfaithful and . . . excuse me . . . he did flaunt that unfaithfulness in a way few wives would put up with."

Selma, flushed with irritation, said, "That's nonsense!"

"I don't think so," Maggie said. "It was a slap in your face, your husband having that party at Miss Daily's suite."

Louie Cohn was starting to rise. "You don't have to listen to this tommyrot, Selma. We were indeed lured here under false pretenses . . ."

Krane was on his feet, too. "I agree with Louie. I like a free steak as much as the next starving artist; but, Maggie, you go too far!"

Even mild Moe Shulman, though he hadn't risen, was objecting. "Miss Starr, you say Mrs. Harrison had a 'reason for resenting' her husband . . . but what you *mean* is, she had a motive."

"Yeah," Harry blurted, "motive for murder!"

Maggie was patting the air with gloved hands. "Please. Please, just a moment. Sit, do please sit, and just listen."

A frozen, awkward pause followed; but finally Louie Cohn, frowning, sat. So did Krane, after heaving a huge put-upon sigh.

"Moe," Maggie said, "Harry . . . you're quite right. I *am* talking about murder motives. And each of you has one, at least for Donny."

"Aw, come on!" Harry said. "How am I any better off with Donny dead? I still have *Louie* to deal with! Or did I spike *his* drink when he wasn't looking?"

Louie, who had no sense of humor, frowned and actually pushed away his half-gone gin fizz.

"Harry," Maggie said, "again, you're right. You really don't have a motive that holds up under scrutiny. And, Moe, you didn't dislike Donny. You and he shared a debilitating disease. He was just about to pay for a surgical procedure, out of his own pocket. You are off the spot. So relax, and wait for your steaks, boys."

Harry made a kind of face, and batted the air, but his relief was apparent; and Moe just leaned back and folded his arms, realizing he was out of danger and enjoying a ringside seat.

Selma, indignant, her face no longer flushed but her neck red as a fire engine, said, "I loved my husband. I did *not* murder him. And I wouldn't risk my life over his, his, his . . . over *her*."

Maggie was nodding. "I don't think you would. You and Donny had what sophisticated Long Island couples call an understanding.

You considered him to be a man of certain needs, some of which you couldn't, or didn't care to, fulfill. That he would have that birthday party at Miss Daily's suite, with you present, shows how confident he was in that understanding. Surely a tactless, thoughtless thing for him to do, even an unforgivable act . . . but probably not one you would murder him over."

Air went out of Selma's indignation; and she, too, seemed to relax.

"As for you, Louie," Maggie said, "your motive for wanting Donny out of the way is a strong one. He represented everything about the comics business that was yesterday; and you foresee a lot of profitable tomorrows for Americana."

Louie, sitting with his arms tightly folded, quietly indignant, mustache twitching, said, "There are many easier, more preferable ways to remove an unwanted business partner than murder. Within the next two years, I would have been able to offer Donny a retirement plan that would give him more money to stay home than to go to work."

Sy Mortimer said, "But Donny loved his work. He *lived* to work."

Louie gave his editor two cold eyes. "Yes, but he was greedy. Something in the inner workings of his little clockwork brain would have chosen in favor of more money for no work. By the time he realized he'd made a mistake, it would be over. The future would be here, and I'd be in charge of it."

Selma, aghast, said, "Louie! What a *horrible* thing to say. . . ."

Suddenly Louie realized how right she was, and he did something uncharacteristically human—he, too, flushed. Nervously, he said, "Forgive me, Selma. The nature of this . . . this half-baked inquisition is such that a blunt answer seemed called for. You know I loved Donny. Loved him like a brother."

Harry said, "Like Cain loved Abel?"

Louie glared at the freelancer, then settled back in his chair. His eyes went to Maggie. "Do you still think I have a motive?"

"Frankly I'm not sure," Maggie said. "You're right that you had other means to dispose of Donny. But I don't imagine you have any moral reservations about murder."

"That's too much!" Louie was on his feet again.

"Sit," she said, as if to a dog. "You didn't kill Donny. You're in the clear, Louie. Just sit and listen. It's to the benefit of all of us— all but one—to clear this thing up, isn't it?"

No one argued with her.

"Louie," Maggie said, "what puts you in the clear is the second murder. You're a lifelong bachelor and have never expressed any interest in women. Where your interests in that department lie, I could not care less. But I don't see you and Honey Daily being any kind of item. So why on earth would you kill her? You wouldn't."

Louie seemed nervous, suddenly; but he stayed seated, and said nothing.

"Sy," she said, "you got yourself in a jam over the *Wonder Boy* fiasco—"

"I did no such thing!" Mortimer yammered.

"Oh," Harry said, "*can* it, Sy! You *know* you blew it."

Maggie said, "Whether you blew it or not, Sy, getting rid of Donny still left you with Louie to deal with . . . and you have a reputation in the business for being a first-rate editor. Everybody makes mistakes, and *Wonder Boy* may be your big one, but I don't think you'll get fired; and I don't think you'd compound that mistake by making the bigger one of committing murder."

"Yes," Mortimer said, shifting in his seat embarrassedly, "well."

"*And* you have absolutely no connection to Honey Daily," Maggie said.

Harry said, "Maybe she saw Sy doctoring Donny's insulin bottle, before the party!"

"Shut up, you pipsqueak!" Mortimer said, half out of his chair and leaning across the table across a centerpiece.

I got off my stool. "Sit down, Sy! *Now.*"

Mortimer looked over at me, and sat.

Maggie said, "Thank you, Jack. And for those of you tonight, who are going to be cleared, I'd like to remind you that the actual detective work was done by my stepson. It's probably too much to ask you to give him a hand, but I just thought I would point that out."

I gave her a little salute and a smile. For some reason, though, nobody applauded.

Maggie said, "Will, I have to admit I really only asked you here tonight to make sure you got a good, substantial meal. Things have been tough on you, lately, but I don't think you blamed Donny for that . . . or if you did, you talked yourself out of it. You're a guy with a wife and a kid that you're hoping to get back in the good graces of . . . killing your boss, and fooling around with your boss's mistress, neither of those would aid you in that effort."

Will Hander smiled, nodded and said, "Wrap it up, would

you, Maggie? The smell of that steak is making my stomach growl."

"I'll do my best, Will," she said with a sparkling smile. "But I do admit you have a motive for murder . . . just not either of the murders that have been committed, so far. But if anyone ever bumps Rod, here, off, well, Will—I will send Jack looking for you."

Krane was on his feet again. "Maggie, this is over the line. Really outrageous. What kind of—"

"What kind of man cheats his partner out of his share? Why, I don't know, Rod. Do you?"

Rod pointed to himself with a thumb. "I sleep good at night. I treat Will just fine, he makes top freelancer dollar . . . doesn't he, Sy? . . . And what any of that has to do with Donny's murder, I haven't the foggiest."

I got up and went over and put a gentle hand on Krane's shoulder. "Be a good boy, Rod. Sit down. Take your medicine. It'll be over soon."

He gave me a look and so I gave him one.

He sat down.

Tell you the truth, everybody knew I was in a mood, and nobody wanted to fool with me. I hadn't been sleeping so good since Honey was killed, and I guess it showed on my face.

I was back on my barstool when Maggie said, "You're quite right, Rod. These murders have nothing to do with comics. The only killing in comic books going on at this table is the money Americana is making, hand over fist, sometimes at the expense of its talent."

Louie Cohn glowered, but stayed mute.

"But you, Rod," she said, and her smile clearly unsettled the *Batwing* creator, "you *are* mixed up in these murders . . . or at least one of them."

The fine nostrils flared. "No! You're out of your redheaded mind! I didn't kill Donny, and I was crazy about Honey!"

Grinning, Harry said, "Crazy enough to kill her?"

Rod swung his head Harry's way. "You shut up, you midget moron! You don't know a goddamn thing about it!"

"None of us," Maggie said, "have known much of anything about Donny's murder, because a basic assumption of ours . . . and of the police . . . has been wrong." She cast a sunny look my way and gestured to me, like a car show model indicating a '49 Jaguar. "Jack—this was *your* discovery. Would you care to share it?"

All faces went to me, heads swiveling on the near side of the table to do so.

I stayed perched on my stool, but spoke up. "The cops weren't interested in the stain on Miss Daily's carpet, a stain as big as Donny himself. But I had a few carpet fibers analyzed. They were heavily doused with poison, that organophosphate Captain Chandler's been talking about."

Harry said, "Yeah, well, why wouldn't it be? You know what a sweating pig Donny was . . . sorry, Selma."

"Donny *was* prone to perspire," I said, demonstrating my delicacy. "And everybody who knew him knew that. I spoke to Captain Chandler yesterday afternoon, about my theory; he called this afternoon and the forensics experts have confirmed it."

Krane, scowling, demanded, "Confirmed *what* in hell?"

"Confirmed that Donny wasn't poisoned by his insulin being

doctored—he wasn't poisoned by injection: he absorbed the poison through his skin . . . from the Wonder Guy costume he was wearing."

Big eyes and murmuring transpired, and Maggie shushed them, then waved a hand to me, to go on.

I did. "As Mrs. Harrison has told us, there was only one Wonder Guy costume, which Donny kept in his possession, for special occasions, parties, conventions, sales conferences. Donny must have announced his intention to those around him that he would be wearing the Wonder Guy suit to his birthday party. Someone in possession of that knowledge took advantage and soaked that super suit in poison."

Moe asked, "Is that possible?"

"Yes." I raised an eyebrow. "And the coroner's office had retained the costume, which had been cut off Donny prior to his autopsy . . . and the police lab now says the material is permeated with that organophosphate."

"The poison," Harry said, with a nod and a shrug. "But what *is* it exactly?"

"Pesticide." I turned toward the man sitting next to me. "The kind of thing a trusted family retainer, who among other things acted as yard boy, would have easy access to. Just as the servant who picked up the family dry cleaning would have easy access to the Wonder Guy costume, as well as the knowledge that Donny planned to wear it to the party."

Hank Morella, in his gray chauffeur's livery, looked pretty gray himself. "That's stupid. I liked Donny. Hell, I loved the guy. Why would I—"

Over at the table, Selma Harrison was insisting, "Jack, you can't be serious! Hank's like a member of the family! He's as loyal as—"

"A family dog?" I suggested. I grinned at Morella, probably not the most attractive grin I ever summoned up. "You were the loyal family chauffeur, the fall guy who years ago took the pornography rap for Donny, and won a menial job for life. Might have seemed like a good deal in the Depression, but it must've lost its luster along the way."

Gray though he was, Morella seemed calm; he remained perched on the stool, an elbow leaning casually on the bar.

"I had no motive," he said. "None. What if you're right . . . and you're *not* . . . that I resented Mr. Harrison, had a grudge against Donny? Why in God's name would I kill him?"

"Not in God's name," I said. "In Honey Daily's."

Now even the gray left, with only white remaining, the same kind of white as the dead skin of a blister.

"I do blame myself," I admitted. "I was slow on the uptake from the start. You dropped by Honey's suite unannounced that morning and said you were stopping by for Donny's things, implying Mrs. Harrison sent you. . . . Selma, did you?"

"Why . . . no. No, of course not. I had no idea Donny kept any, any 'things' at that awful woman's place."

Morella said nothing. Just stared at me, unblinking, and white.

"You were just covering for yourself," I said. "You were there to see Honey. And she seemed irritated to see you. Meantime, you were shocked to see me, and not at all happy . . . since I'd obviously spent the night. You were another one of the men in Honey's life, Hank . . . only you thought you were the *only* man . . . the only man beside Donny, that is. You remove him, you kill this disgusting beast, knowing that Honey will remain on the Americana payroll for years to come, clearing the way for youself. You loved her, didn't you?"

Morella swallowed.

"You just didn't know you were one of several men she juggled at a time." I grunted a laugh. "You didn't even know about *Rod*, did you?" I spoke to Krane without taking my eyes off the chauffeur. "Rod, you might have been a murder victim, at that, if the cards had fallen differently. But you knew about Hank, here, didn't you? That he was another of the men in Honey's little black book?"

Krane's voice was small and pitiful, a bleat: "Y-yes."

"And Rod," I said, still looking at Morella, "you even *told* me about him, didn't you? But you were too cute about it and I was too dumb—you said Honey was involved with 'maybe the most powerful man' at Americana. You didn't mean a bigwig, like I assumed, Rod—you meant *literally* powerful, like Mr. Beefcake of 1943, here."

Morella's eyes tightened, just barely.

"And when I told you that," I said to the chauffeur, "when I casually referred to Rod and all the various men in Honey's life, you went a little crazy, didn't you, big fella?"

"You should stop now," Morella said quietly.

"First you called some old friends of yours, back when you were connected to the mob, like your benefactor Donny was once upon a time. Guys who, like you, used to work for Frank Calabria. You told them to tail me, and work me over, and warn me off. But, damnit, I didn't pay attention to their warning—if I was being strong-armed off the case, why would these goons tell me to 'Stay away from *her*!' Only . . . I wasn't just looking into the case, and maybe targeting your behind for Old Sparky at Sing Sing . . . no, I was another of the men you didn't want in Honey's life."

"That's enough," he said.

"And then, with the gears in your noggin still not meshing right, you went over to the Waldorf, to her suite, and of course you got right in . . . and you confronted her about it, about all these men, and she probably said it was none of your damn business, and maybe finally you told her what you'd done for her, but she wasn't impressed, was she? Or, anyway, not in the way you'd hoped she'd be. And she disappointed you. Disappointed you so bad that you took her not in your arms but in your hands, and squeezed the life out of that funny, sad, smart, beautiful woman."

"I thought she was wonderful," he said softly, through clenched teeth. "But she was a tramp! A filthy whore. My only regret is . . . I can't kill her again. And again! And again!"

"Once was enough," I said.

And my remark was enough, too, because he did just what I was hoping he'd do: jump at me.

I couldn't kill him. I promised Maggie no vigilante nonsense. But I owed Honey this much: I broke that square superhero jaw with one sharp, hard swing.

The roll of quarters helped.

He fell to the floor by the bar, not unconscious, but out of commission. And then he did the damnedest thing: he started to cry.

And for a small, very infinitesimal slice of a second, I did the damnedest thing: I felt sorry for him.

But it passed so quick I barely noticed, and then Chandler was by my side, come up from the back where he'd been running the three tape recorders he'd set up this afternoon, two hidden mikes at the table, one at the bar.

"Get what you need?" I asked him.

"Oh yeah," he said, with a nasty grin, hauling Morella up off the floor. Another plainclothes dick, a colored guy, was pulling the chauffeur's hands behind him, to properly cuff him.

As they dragged the murderer out—they forgot his chauffeur's cap, and I kept it as a souvenir—I headed over to the banquet-style table where all eyes were large and all jaws were gaping, like something out of the damn comics . . . except for Maggie's. She was hooded-eyed and beautiful and gently smiling; at some point in my part of the proceedings, she'd sat herself down.

"Well done, Jack," she said, and touched my sleeve. "Well done."

"Christ, I hope not," I said. "I want mine with some juice in it—medium rare, at least. . . . Let's eat."

And everybody except Louis Cohn stayed for the free feed-sack. He could afford to pay, and preferred to pick his own company.

I wish I could report happy endings all around, but the *Funny Guy* strip bombed, the comic book, too. And, after a bunch of strained courtroom claptrap, on the advice of their lawyer,

Spiegel and Shulman settled for one hundred grand, most of which Bert Zelman's fees ate up, and Americana did not offer them a new contract. *Wonder Guy* flew on without them.

Funny thing—within the year, attorney Zelman set himself up as a Hollywood producer; he did a bunch of Mamie Van Doren pictures, all rotten (I know—I saw every one). Where Zelman got the kind of dough to produce movies, only God knows, or maybe Louie Cohn. What would it have been worth, under the table, do you suppose, to make the *Wonder Guy* boys disappear?

Meanwhile, as we say in the funnies, Rod Krane's underage ploy worked, and he got a big fat contract and continual solo by-line credit, while Will Hander went on freelancing for small change. The '60s *Batwing* TV show made Krane very wealthy, and he exhibited pop art paintings that were probably ghosted, though they were lousy enough to be his. The campy TV show based many of its episodes on Will Hander scripts, without credit or compensation. He died broke, without his family, and probably drunk. Comics historians consider him the co-creator of the famous caped crimefighter, but Rod, who died rich and somewhat famous, still gets the official credit.

Selma Harrison died just shy of ten years later, of a heart attack, out on the patio where we spoke.

Louis Cohn got onto the board of directors of the huge corporation that bought Americana in the '70s, and died at age one hundred. That's a long time for a bastard like Louie to live, but think of it this way: one hundred years of humorless boredom is a kind of prison in itself.

Speaking of which, Hank Morella went to Sing Sing, as I predicted, and indeed got the hot seat. The papers had lost interest by that time, though. Love-nest murders were a dime a dozen in New York in those days, and the newshounds had been counting on a killer from the comic business (and come to think of it, that would have been the only way a syndicated cartoonist could land on the front page).

You probably know that in their later life, Spiegel and Shulman—thanks to the lobbying of a younger generation of comic-book professionals—embarrassed Americana's new corporate owners into giving the two aging creators substantial pensions. Spiegel had been reduced to civil service clerking, and Shulman was blind, living with his family back in Des Moines.

But the blockbuster *Wonder Guy* motion picture—one of the top-grossing movies of the 1970s—had their names in the opening credits, big and bold, right up on the screen: *Created by Harry Spiegel and Moe Shulman*. And it must have meant a hell of a lot to the boys.

Too bad Moe couldn't see it.

A TIP OF THE FEDORA

This novel, despite some obvious parallels to events in the history of the comics medium, is fiction. It employs characters with real-life counterparts as well as composites and wholly fictional ones.

Unlike previous historical novels of mine—the Nathan Heller "memoirs," the Eliot Ness series, the "disaster" mysteries and the *Road* trilogy—I have chosen not to use real names and/or to hew religiously to actual events. As this is a mystery in the Rex Stout or Ellery Queen tradition, the murder herein has only the vaguest historical basis, and real-life conflicts have been heightened and exaggerated while others are wholly fabricated. Characters reminiscent of real people, in particular cartoonists and editors and others in the comics industry of the 1940s, are portrayed unflatteringly at times, because they are, after all, meant to be the suspects in a murder mystery.

While I invite readers—particularly comics fans—to enjoy the roman à clef aspect of *A Killing in Comics*, I caution them not to view this as history but as the fanciful (if fact-inspired) novel it is.

That said, I wish to in particular acknowledge Gerard Jones for his masterful, compelling *Men of Tomorrow* (2004), which tells the true story behind my imaginary tale. Jones has said kind things about *Ms. Tree*, the comic book created by myself and Terry Beatty—who provides the illustrations for this novel—and I now owe him twice over.

For New York color I leaned upon *New York: Confidential* (1948) by Jack Lait and Lee Mortimer; and the WPA Guide for New York City (1939).

My longtime research associate George Hagenauer provided me with hundreds of pages of photocopies from various issues of fanzines (in particular, *The Comics Journal*, *Comic Book Artist* and *Alter Ego*) featuring interviews with writers and artists of the Golden Age of comic books. My thanks to George, and to the fanzines and their scribes who work so diligently to record the history of the comics medium.

Other books consulted included *The Mad World of William M. Gaines* (1972), Frank Jacobs; and *Batman and Me* (1989), Bob Kane with Tom Andrae. I also drew upon reminiscences of the early days of comic books shared with me by writer Mickey Spillane, who passed away during the writing of the final chapters of this novel.

Thanks to editor Natalee Rosenstein for her patience and support, and for suggesting that I use the world of comics as the backdrop for a mystery; my agent and friend Dominick Abel; and my wife Barbara, my invaluable in-house line editor.

MAX ALLAN COLLINS, a Mystery Writers of America Edgar® nominee in both fiction and nonfiction categories, was hailed in 2005 by *Publishers Weekly* as "a new breed of writer." He has earned an unprecedented fourteen Private Eye Writers of America "Shamus" nominations for his historical thrillers, winning twice for his Nathan Heller novels, *True Detective* (1983) and *Stolen Away* (1991), and in 2006 received the PWA "Eye" for Life Achievement.

His other credits include film criticism, short fiction, songwriting, trading-card sets, and movie/TV tie-in novels, including *Air Force One*, *In the Line of Fire*, and the *New York Times*–bestselling *Saving Private Ryan*. His nonfiction work includes *The History of Mystery*, nominated for every major mystery award, and the Anthony-winning *Men's Adventure Magazines*, cowritten by George Hagenauer.

His graphic novel *Road to Perdition* is the basis of the Academy Award–winning DreamWorks 2002 feature film starring Tom Hanks, Paul Newman and Jude Law, directed by Sam Mendes. His many comics credits include the *Dick Tracy* syndicated strip (1977–1993); *Ms. Tree* (created by Collins and artist Terry Beatty); *Batman*; and *CSI: Crime Scene Investigation*, based on the hit TV series for which he has also written video games, jigsaw puzzles, and a *USA Today*–bestselling series of novels.

An independent filmmaker in his native Iowa, he wrote and directed *Mommy*, premiering on Lifetime in 1996, as well as a 1997 sequel, *Mommy's Day*. The screenwriter of *The Expert*, a 1995 HBO World Premiere, he wrote and directed the innovative made-for-DVD feature, *Real Time: Siege at Lucas Street Market* (2000). *Shades of Noir* (2004) is an anthology of his short films, including his award-winning documentary, *Mike Hammer's Mickey Spillane*. He recently completed a feature-length documentary, *Caveman: V. T. Hamlin and Alley Oop*, and the film version of his Edgar-nominated play, *Eliot Ness: An Untouchable Life*, took top honors at two regional film festivals in 2006.

Collins lives in Muscatine, Iowa, with his wife, writer Barbara Collins, sometimes collaborating under the name "Barbara Allan." Their son Nathan is an honors graduate in computer science and Japanese at the University of Iowa at nearby Iowa City, and recently completed postgrad studies in Japan.